"What do you have to do with the disappearance of Leonardo Chastain?"

Julia stared hard at him, the weaker part of herself wanting to believe him, wanting to think he was as he portrayed himself.

Keys in her fist, arranged as a weapon with one poling out between each finger, she faced him and said, "If you take one more step—"

He stopped, holding up his hands. He smiled then—the first smile she'd seen. If he thought she was one of those women who rolled over when a handsome man smiled at her, he was in for a surprise.

"Julia, I came here to see you. I came to get Leo back."

She couldn't remember giving him her name. "Get him back? If you didn't know he was going to be kidnapped then how—"

"I didn't know about the kidnapping. I came to get him back...from you."

"From me?"

"Of course I came for him. I'm his father."

ALICE SHARPE

ROYAL HEIR

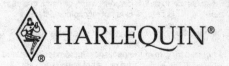

TORONTO • NEW YORK • LONDON
AMSTERDAM • PARIS • SYDNEY • HAMBURG
STOCKHOLM • ATHENS • TOKYO • MILAN • MADRID
PRAGUE • WARSAW • BUDAPEST • AUCKLAND

This book is dedicated to my friends in the
Mid-Willamette Valley RWA whose
professionalism, enthusiasm and giant hearts
make a solitary job so much more fun.
Round trip tickets to Montivitz for everyone!

ISBN-13: 978-0-373-88796-5
ISBN-10:   0-373-88796-5

ROYAL HEIR

Copyright © 2007 by Alice Sharpe

This edition published by arrangement with Harlequin Books S.A.

® and TM are trademarks of the publisher. Trademarks indicated with
® are registered in the United States Patent and Trademark Office, the
Canadian Trade Marks Office and in other countries.

www.eHarlequin.com

Printed in U.S.A.

ABOUT THE AUTHOR

Alice Sharpe met her husband-to-be on a cold, foggy beach in Northern California. One year later they were married. Their union has survived the rearing of two children, a handful of earthquakes registering over 6.5, numerous cats and a few special dogs, the latest of which is a yellow Lab named Annie Rose. Alice and her husband now live in a small rural town in Oregon, where she devotes the majority of her time to pursuing her second love, writing.

Alice loves to hear from readers. You can write her at P.O. Box 755, Brownsville, OR 97327. A SASE for reply is appreciated.

Books by Alice Sharpe

HARLEQUIN INTRIGUE
746—FOR THE SAKE OF THEIR BABY
823—UNDERCOVER BABIES
923—MY SISTER, MYSELF*
929—DUPLICATE DAUGHTER*
1022—ROYAL HEIR

*Dead Ringer

CAST OF CHARACTERS

William "Will" Chastain—Is it possible his mysterious past is catching up with him? Why else is everyone he loves either missing or dead? Now it's his son's life that he must save before it's too late.

Julia Sheridan—Her difficult childhood taught her not to trust too early. She's denied the leisure of time when the baby she loves disappears and the man sworn to find that child rises from the dead.

Nicole Chastain—Will's beautiful, self-absorbed wife. Her final affair appears to be the catalyst for mayhem...and what may have led to her untimely death.

Monsieur Henri Pepin—The last known person to see Leo Chastain. Was the dapper lawyer duped or was he part of the kidnapping plot?

George Abbot—Is Julia's boss's help free or is there an ultimate price to pay?

Fiona Chastain—Why has Will's eccentric aunt persisted in keeping Will in the dark even after he's reached adulthood?

Minister Poletier—Is this plodding bureaucrat's most egregious sin his loyalty to crown and throne?

King Theodore Lévesque—Years before, this monarch set things in motion that now threaten his monarchy. Is he evil enough to plot his own son's death?

Paul Bernard—A rebel leader out to liberate an entire country, no matter what the cost.

Prologue

The call came as he prepared to leave the office. He had to scramble to get the phone himself as his secretary had left for the day and the damn thing was hidden under a sheet of architectural drawings.

The caller's voice caught him at once, though, her anxiety as loud and clear as her voice was furtive.

"I've got compromising photos of your wife and my husband. He'll kill me if he finds out I hired a private detective to follow him. I'm too scared to use the pictures myself, but the bastard deserves to be humiliated. The pictures are yours if you want them… just be careful. He's chief of police…"

She'd gone on to name a waterside restaurant across the river. She'd get her sister to drive her there. "Meet me in one hour…"

By now he was living on his boat, a thirty-two-foot cruiser with two powerful gasoline engines, and his mind raced as he plotted a course across the river. Her last murmured, "Make sure you aren't followed," trailed him all the way down to the marina as he threw cautious glances in the rearview mirror.

He'd known his wife was seeing someone but the chief of police? Who *was* the chief of police, anyway?

The big engines started at once and he cast off the dock lines without fanfare, replacing his tailored suit jacket with a heavy wool coat as April was cold this far north. He'd crossed the river many, many times, often after sundown. He kept his gaze on the buoys and distant landmarks. He knew the channel, was comfortable with the strong currents. He was an experienced, methodical boater.

But in his mind, the caller's frantic voice tangled with the memory of his wife's. She'd promised to ruin him, to take his child…

Not if he could help it.

Revealing, embarrassing pictures might be enough to get her to back down...it was a chance worth taking.

He heard the other vessel before he saw it, a distant buzz that grew louder even though no lights shone on the water. He turned off his own cockpit light, thinking it might be robbing him of night vision, and then he saw it, a black hull, low freeboard, racing toward him like a SCUD missile.

He blinked his running lights back on and flipped the switches of every other light he could reach until his yacht shone like a Christmas tree. Still the smaller boat raced toward him. Mesmerized, it took him too long to admit he was the target, that if he didn't do something right now he was going to be blown out of the water.

Climbing up on the stern gunwale, he dove into the black river, taking deep, strong pulls with his arms to move as far away from his own propeller and the impending explosion as possible. The coat weighed him down, slowed him down and he slipped his arms free as he surfaced. At that moment, the two vessels collided, filling the night air with fire and smoke.

Debris rained down, falling close by,

scorching his face and hair, sending him back below the surface to the quiet depths of water too cold to keep a man alive for long.

Chapter One

April 11, San Francisco, California

With an anxious glance at the clock on her dashboard, Julia Sheridan pulled into the San Francisco airport short-term parking garage. She was more than an hour late, her margin for safety eaten up by a flat tire and the bumbling Good Samaritan who had stopped to "help" her.

As if she couldn't change her own tire.

The first empty parking spot she found was four flights up and toward the back. She was out of the car in a flash, hair, jeans and leather flight jacket damp from her adventure beside the freeway. Straightening the white wool scarf around her neck and slinging her huge shoulder bag over her arm, she hurried toward the elevator, heart pounding in anticipation.

Once aboard the elevator, she slid to the side and took her cell phone from her coat pocket, punching in the lawyer's number. As before, she was directed to leave a message but this time she didn't bother.

She should have given herself more time for potential problems. As an air transport pilot, who knew better than she the inevitable last-minute crisis that threw the best-laid plans awry? But she'd been rushing around this Saturday morning like nobody's business, buying baby furniture and diapers, a car seat and special shampoo. Even the stuffed blue elephant she'd left on the passenger seat of the car still sported tags dangling from one floppy ear.

The elevator made the ground floor in seconds. As she made her way through the crowd waiting to get on the elevator, she spied several families with small children and her heart lurched. One woman with deep-set eyes and long, dark hair clutched a blanketed baby to her chest while a tall man in a raincoat put a protective arm around her shoulders.

Julia was riddled with self-doubt. Without a husband, could she make a family for Leo? Would she be enough?

The twinge in her heart was replaced by a vow: she would be all the family little Leo ever needed.

She'd spoken to the lawyer two or three times in the week since Nicole's death, each time struggling to understand the lawyer's thick French-Canadian accent. He'd emigrated from Quebec to Seattle years earlier, he'd explained, but the accent was part of him and he couldn't seem to shake it. He'd told her she would recognize him by his dark mustache and bald head.

She also assumed he'd be one of very few men holding a ten-month-old baby.

As she hurried toward the gate where he'd told her he'd wait, she found herself crossing her fingers that he was a patient man, that he wouldn't have given up and caught a flight back home or that Leo wouldn't be howling…

She found the lawyer with no trouble, his mustache small and tidy. He wore a camel-hair coat over a black suit, his shoes as polished as his balding dome. He sat on a chair near the windows, a briefcase on his lap, a book in his hand, which he seemed to be studying. There was no sign of Nicole's baby.

Your baby now.

Julia came to a stop in front of him. "Monsieur Henri Pepin?" she gasped.

Lowering the engagement diary, he looked up at her with round, brown eyes. *"Oui."*

"I'm Nicole Chastain's cousin."

The man blinked a couple of times. His gaze raking her up and down, expression guarded, he said, "Mademoiselle?"

Julia finger-combed long, damp, dark tendrils away from her face, tendrils that had escaped her habitual ponytail. Assuming his hesitation had something to do with the fact that she looked more like a drowned rat than a soon-to-be guardian of her cousin's baby, she added, "My tire blew. On the interstate. Some klutz stopped to help… It's raining out there and windy. Anyway, I tried calling to tell you I was running late, but—"

"My phone is not on," he said. "It was not necessary to turn it on."

"Didn't you wonder where I was?"

"But, no, mademoiselle. I was met at the gate as planned. Most expedient."

Julia sank down on the chair beside him. She said, "I don't understand. Where's Leo?"

He looked as confused as she felt. He said,

"Nor do I. You are Nicole Chastain's cousin? She had another?"

"No, no, just the one, just me, Julia Sheridan, Leonardo's guardian as named in Nicole's will. You called me, monsieur, the day after her death, six days ago. You said since Nicole's husband died last month—"

"*Oui,* in a boating accident. Most unfortunate."

"Yes. Well, you told me Nicole wanted me to become Leo's guardian. You said you would bring him to me as instructed in her will. Where is he? Where's Leo?"

Now his mouth was as round as his eyes. "Yes, yes, this is all true, but there must be some misunderstanding. I was met right here. By Julia Sheridan."

"I'm sorry?"

"Julia Sheridan was waiting for me when I arrived." He narrowed his eyes before adding, "She is different than you but much the same. Her voice is lower, her speech more formal. Her fiancé is a fine fellow. Quiet." With a scolding expression as though he disapproved of Julia's attempt at a hoax, he added, "I assure you, she had all the right papers."

Julia swallowed the knot in her throat. "But I'm Julia Sheridan."

They stared at each other for a long moment until Julia felt another gaze boring into her back. She turned to catch a tall, well-built man glancing away.

He appeared to be in his early thirties, black hair, gray eyes, dressed in an ill-fitting gray suit. His gaze followed a parade of straggling teenagers with the studied indifference of a policeman.

The lawyer said, "Mademoiselle?"

Blinking, Julia looked back at Pepin. "Do you mean that you gave Leo to someone pretending to be me?"

Trembling now, the lawyer opened his briefcase and shuffled through the contents. "Here, here," he protested, shoving papers complete with Julia's signature. Only it wasn't Julia's handwriting, but how was he supposed to know that?

"When did this happen?" she asked, her voice rising in alarm.

He glanced at his watch. "The other… Julia…she left a half hour ago. Maybe a few minutes more. She took the infant, Leonardo Chastain, with her."

Julia opened her shoulder bag and brought

out all the identification she had been told she would need to verify her identity: social security card, birth certificate, passport, driver's license. She'd even included a picture of herself taken with Nicole a few weeks before. In the photo, Julia held Leo as Nicole hadn't wanted to take a chance the baby would spit up on her dress. Julia shoved the photo beneath a protesting Henri Pepin's nose.

He blinked as he studied the image of Julia—brown hair tamed into a long pony-tail, no makeup, grinning—and Nicole—flaming red hair, hips thrust forward, shoulders back, expression grim. Julia recalled the conversation preceding the photo snapped by one of Julia's friends. Nicole had been complaining about her soon-to-be ex-husband, saying how tight-fisted he was, how mean, how he was going to rue the day he met her.

The lawyer gasped. *"Mon dieu!"* he said, as tiny beads of perspiration popped out on his high forehead. "How can this be?"

Julia echoed the sentiment as she rifled through his copies of what appeared to be legal documents and photocopies of fake identification.

"Why?" she insisted. "Why would anyone go to such lengths to claim Leo?"

"There is no reason. He is just an ordinary baby. His parents, before their deaths, ordinary people, a little savings, a little debt…"

"Who knew you were bringing him here?" Julia added.

"My office, child protection, the police. It was even in the newspaper. It was no secret."

"Monsieur Pepin, we need to alert security at once. We need to find Leo."

"Oui, oui," the lawyer said, snapping his case shut again and rising.

Julia was already on her feet. "Tell me again what the woman looked like," she pleaded as they hurried toward a uniformed airline employee.

"Much like you, mademoiselle," the lawyer said, his accent growing thicker as his panic escalated. "The man, I don't know, very quiet," he added. "Fair complexion, name of George Abbot, wearing a raincoat…"

"George Abbot?" Julia asked, forehead wrinkled.

"Oui. I had wrapped the baby in a white blanket…"

Julia pushed away the alarm that her boss's name had produced as she recalled the people getting on the elevator as she got off. Man with blond hair, much like the real George Abbot, but too tall, too thin, baby bundled in a light-colored, perhaps white, blanket, its face hidden against the woman's shoulder, deep-set brown eyes on the woman herself.

Eyes like Julia's.

With Monsieur Pepin's voice ringing in her ears, Julia darted off down the bustling corridor. "Call the police," she yelled as she shouldered her way through the crush.

Someone grabbed her arm. She twirled and faced the man she'd noticed earlier. The one in the gray suit. He blurted out, "What is it? What's wrong?"

Julia did not like strangers touching her or asking questions that were none of their business. But there was a look in this man's eyes that stopped her from rebuffing him. Besides, she was scared to death her tardiness had put Leo's life in jeopardy and this guy looked official. She said, "A kidnapping. My baby—"

"Your baby?" the man said, and now there was something new in his eyes and she felt a new wave of apprehension.

"It's too difficult to explain. Let go of me, I need to search—"

"I'll go with you," he said.

"Who are you?"

"Airport security," he snapped as he dropped his hand. "Quick, tell me what happened."

Julia related the facts. As she spoke, they hurried to the elevator, retracing her steps, scouring the elevator when it emptied of people, searching each floor of the parking garage, looking in among the sea of cars for a tall blond man, a woman with dark eyes, a ten-month-old baby in a white blanket.

"It's useless," Julia cried as they reentered the airport. She faced the fact that the couple could have transferred to a different terminal, boarded a private plane.

A knot of uniforms surrounded the lawyer. Julia's heart leapt in a surge of hope.

"Maybe they found him," the man said.

Julia called out, "Monsieur Pepin? Is Leo safe?"

As one, the crowd turned to face Julia. "No, no," Monsieur Pepin said, his face now pale, his voice jittery. "There is no sign, I'm afraid. He's vanished into thin air."

A huge man with tiny glasses perched on

his nose and white-blond hair parted in the middle strode toward Julia. "San Francisco police," he said, flipping open a badge. "Detective Morris. I need to ask you a few questions, Miss Sheridan. Let's start with why you ran off."

"I remembered seeing three people fitting the descriptions Monsieur Pepin gave me," Julia said, her voice shaky and it wasn't just because of Leo. Standing face-to-face, more or less, with a uniformed police officer who towered over her made her feel small and vulnerable. "I thought there might be time to catch them in the garage. This gentleman—" She paused here, turning to face the man who'd been helping her, hoping to enlist his aid in this explanation but he'd disappeared. She glanced in a full circle—he was gone.

"Miss Sheridan?"

"Where did the guy from airport security go?"

"Airport security is fanning out all over the airport. I need to ask you a few questions."

Julia's head threatened to explode. Years of helplessness, of being shuffled between foster homes, of never being in control, never belonging, never understanding, never being able to count on anyone or anything came charging back.

"Miss Sheridan?" The detective's voice sounded softer this time.

"Leo's gone," she said, tears flooding her eyes as she gazed up at him. "Oh, my heavens, he's gone."

Detective Morris took her arm and guided her to a plastic chair. She closed her eyes. Leo had been her chance to make the world a better place for one small, orphaned child.

And she'd failed him.

HOURS LATER, after answering a million questions, Julia made her way back to her car.

She attempted to make a mental list. George Abbot needed to be alerted—there would be questions asked of him, embarrassing questions about why anyone would pretend he and Julia were engaged. And the babysitter she'd arranged to watch Leo on Monday morning when she had to fly a load of computer parts to Fresno had to be cancelled. Unless Leo was back by then, unless his kidnappers returned him—

Face it: the hoax was too elaborate for an easy resolution. Someone had gone to a lot of trouble to take Leo. The police expected a ransom call and had arranged to tap her home phone. She was directed to keep a close account of all incoming cell phone transmissions.

She had to shake this fuzzy feeling that made each step an effort. She had to get past the horror of what had happened and work on a solution.

Trouble was, Julia didn't have anything to ransom. She owed money on her car, on her house, on every credit card. She had no rich family—for that matter, no family at all now that Nicole was dead. She had several friends but they were poor, too. Except for George Abbot, but he was her boss and his money was tied up in his company. The bank would laugh in her face if she asked for a loan.

How was she ever going to find Leo and get him back? Oh, why had her tire blown out this morning of all mornings? Why had she been so polite to the man who had been determined to put the spare on for her? Why hadn't she told him to get lost, that she'd do it herself? Why hadn't she given herself more time? What good was baby furniture without a baby?

Worse thoughts crept into her head as she exited the elevator and started toward her car. Was Leo okay? Would the kidnappers take good care of him? At least he was too young to identify them. The worries circled around in her head like vultures over carrion.

One thing was more or less certain. The child was no longer at the airport. All exiting vehicles and departing flights had been searched but the time delay between his disappearance and the start of the investigation meant there had been plenty of time for Leo's kidnappers to whisk him away in a car or even on a plane if the timing was good. The police would check every flight manifesto, looking for an unexplained babe in arms, but Julia had a feeling it would all be in vain. Whoever took him was a wizard with identification papers—Leo would be well documented under a phony name. Anyone could claim Leo was theirs. Who would ever suspect?

She'd never before considered how vulnerable a baby was. He couldn't talk for himself. If he cried, his kidnappers would pat him on the back and onlookers would think he was just fussy. Without fingerprinting or DNA samples, Leo was a ten-month-old

Caucasian boy just like any other ten-month-old Caucasian boy. He had a little strawberry mark on the back of his neck, but who would see that with blankets pulled up around his head?

Even in the dim light of the parking garage she could see ahead to her car and discern the fuzzy raised blue trunk of the huge stuffed elephant she'd bought to welcome Leo. That elephant had been her version of a promise: *Everything will be okay. I'll make it okay.*

Tears filled her eyes. The emptiness of her arms mirrored the big hole in her heart.

The sound of a car engine revving broke through her thoughts. She looked up to find two headlights bearing down on her. In the next instant, someone tackled her from the right. She felt as much as heard a dull thud as she flew, still trapped in her tackler's arms, until they landed on the pavement, his body cushioning hers. She looked up to see two red taillights turning the corner toward the exit ramp.

The man spent little time righting himself and dragging Julia to her feet as well. The fall had knocked the breath out of her.

She looked up to find clear gray eyes, eyes

she'd seen just hours before as he helped her search for Leo.

"Are you okay?" he said.

She tore herself from his grip. "You!"

"Listen—"

"No," she said, stepping away from him, brushing off her clothes, ashamed of the way her hands trembled. "You're not with airport security, are you?"

Wincing, he mumbled, "No."

Noticing the tear in the sleeve of his suit and the blood-streaked white shirt beneath, she said, "You're hurt. The car hit you."

"It doesn't matter," he said.

She took off her wool scarf and wrapped it around his arm. "You need to get it cleaned and disinfected."

His face reflected none of the pain the gash must have inflicted. He said, "It's nothing."

Tucking one end of the scarf under the makeshift bandage, she narrowed her eyes. "What do you have to do with the disappearance of Leonardo Chastain?"

"Nothing, I swear," he said.

She stared hard at him, the weaker part of herself wanting to believe him, wanting to think he was as he portrayed himself. But he'd already lied to her.

She said, "I was late today picking up Leo because some doofus on the freeway stopped to help me when my tire blew. I couldn't get rid of him and he didn't know what he was doing. And then right after I found out Leo was gone, you appeared and led me on a merry chase up and down the elevator—"

"*I* led *you?*" he said. "You were the one leading."

"And now Leo is gone and you show up again—"

"You're forgetting the car that came within inches of killing you just now," he said, his voice tight. "The one I saved you from." Brow wrinkled, he addressed his next comments to himself. "I don't get it," he mumbled. "*Who* was driving that car?"

"A bad driver—"

"I don't think so. I've been watching you since you got off the elevator and began walking this way. You've been preoccupied. That car came out of the shadows, headed straight for you. And that doesn't fit—"

Julia, digging in her shoulder bag for her keys, kept moving toward her car, aware he followed. She zeroed in on the blue elephant. "Fit what?" she said.

No answer.

Keys in her fist, arranged as a weapon with one poking out between each finger, she faced him. She said, "If you take one more step—"

He stopped, holding up his hands. He smiled then—the first smile she'd seen. If he thought she was one of those women who rolled over when a handsome man smiled at them he was in for a surprise. Julia had been smiled at many times by men she didn't know and seldom had anything good come of it. But then she'd been weaker, smaller, more frightened—a victim. She reached inside herself, reclaiming the gutsy broad she'd had to become to survive. "Go away," she said.

"Julia, listen to me."

She couldn't remember giving him her name. It jarred her into mumbling, "I'm listening."

"I came here to see you. I came to get Leo back."

"I knew you were in on this!" she said, tightening her grip on the keys.

"You don't understand," he said.

"How can I understand? You haven't said anything."

He looked down at his feet and then at her. Eyes smoldering with an intensity that unnerved her, he repeated, "I came to get Leo back."

"Get him back? If you didn't know he was going to be kidnapped then how—"

"I didn't know about the kidnapping. I came to get him back…from you."

"From me?"

Staring into her eyes, he added, "Of course I came for him. I'm his father."

Chapter Two

Julia absorbed this latest shock for a moment before mumbling, "Are you saying that the late William Chastain wasn't Leo's father?"

"No. I'm telling you that *I* am William Chastain."

"He's dead," Julia said.

"Well, no."

"Nicole called me the week before she died and told me he was killed when his boat blew up."

"And his body?"

"Between the explosion and the river currents, what body?"

"Exactly. I know it's hard for you to believe, but I didn't die on the river. I escaped."

Julia shook her head. "Preposterous. Why would Nicole say you were dead if you weren't?"

"Because she didn't know I wasn't."

Julia shook her head again. "This is crazy—"

"I know it sounds nuts. But I can explain."

"So do it."

"Not here."

She stared at him.

"Listen, Leo has big blue eyes and fuzzy reddish hair, like his mother. Like she had. He has a little mark on the back of his neck, a birthmark. You're Julia Sheridan, Nicole's cousin. You've just known Nicole a couple of years. I believe she took advantage of your generosity by calling on you to watch Leo when she flew down here to party with her pals. Am I close?"

"Close," Julia said. "Trouble is, the people who took Leo knew all about me, too."

"Then ask me something unique about Nicole."

Julia rubbed her temples. Would this confusion never stop? She looked into his eyes and once again resisted the pull to trust him, to take him at face value. She said, "Why don't you just show me some identification?"

He smiled again, but this time the thought crossed her mind that the gesture was fueled by frustration. "I don't have any identification," he said. "My wallet was in my suit jacket when my boat blew up. I wasn't wearing it at the time."

"Of course you weren't," she said.

He waved aside her sarcasm. "If I understood what was happening in there with the lawyer, the kidnappers produced all sorts of fake documents, right? If I was one of them, don't you think I'd at least have made myself a nice official-looking Washington state driver's license?"

He had a point.

"Look at me," he added.

She did as he asked and for the first time, she noticed the details that she'd been too preoccupied to notice before.

"What happened to you?" she said. "Why are you wearing someone else's clothes? What happened to your forehead and cheeks? When's the last time you slept?"

"The clothes belong to some poor guy who left his car unlocked and his dry cleaning in the backseat."

"You stole a suit?"

"I just wish he'd been a taller man," he said and they both glanced down at the pant legs, which were too short. The sleeves were, too.

"What about those marks on your face? And your hair…?"

"The marks are leftover burns from the boat explosion. The hair got burned, too. Not too bad, but it frizzled off in spots."

Julia suppressed a sigh. Things just kept getting more and more bizarre.

"After the crash, I managed to swim to shore. I had a friend with an old cabin cruiser in a small marina. He's out of town. I jimmied the lock on his boat and hunkered down to figure things out."

"Why? Why not just go home?"

"Because my home blew up. I wasn't living with Nicole by then. And I suspected she might have had a hand in trying to kill me."

"Why would you—"

"Later. Right now, you're the one in danger. Someone tried to run you down a few minutes ago. It doesn't fit with what I think happened to Leo, but maybe there are two different agendas at work or maybe your boyfriend went postal—"

"Don't be absurd."

"You think he's too stable? You never know—"

"I don't have a boyfriend."

He rubbed the back of his neck with his hand, wincing as the muscle in his upper arm flexed. "Do you think we could get out of here and go somewhere a little less…open?" he said.

"I need to go home. I need to be there to answer the phone."

"Why?"

"The police think someone will call with a ransom—"

"No," he said.

"What do you mean?"

"If my suspicions are right, Leo is in no danger of being hurt. There'll never be a ransom call. The danger will be that he'll all but disappear off the face of the earth. We have to move fast."

She studied his eyes for a second then swore under her breath. She wanted to believe him. She wanted Leo to be safe, but how? "I don't understand. You know who kidnapped him?"

"I have my suspicions."

"Then tell me. Tell the cops or the FBI. Why are we standing here talking—"

"Because I'm not going to tell anyone anything until I use a phone and make certain."

"I have a cell phone—"

"It's not that easy. Finding the right number is going to take a little work."

"Listen," she said, turning again to the car, "it's been a long day and I'm tired of your riddles. I'm going home."

"I don't think that's a good idea," he said.

Bristling, Julia whirled to face him. "What do you mean by that?"

"I mean someone just tried to mow you down."

"So you say."

"Your house might be the next place they try."

She swallowed a jolt of fear. Her house was her refuge. The thought someone might breach it—

"Go to a friend's house for the night," he said.

"I can't. I have to be there if the kidnappers call."

"But—"

"I can't bet on your suspicions even if I understood them, which I don't. I'm going home."

"Then I'll go with you."

"Hold on," she said. If this man was Nicole's husband, he was turning out to be just as infuriating as her cousin had always insisted he was. Julia didn't have the time or energy for any more verbal sparring. Time was passing, Leo was gone…

She added, "I don't want you to come to my house. If you follow me, I'll drive straight to the police station—"

"I can't follow anyone right now," he said. "I hitchhiked down here when I read that Leo was being sent to you. I was lucky to make it to the airport on time. Come on, Julia, think. There must be something about Nicole that wouldn't make its way onto a fact sheet and would convince you I was married to her. Some habit, some gesture. Like the way she flipped that mane of hair. The way her eyes could turn you to stone when she was unhappy with you. The obsession with red underwear, the mole on her left thigh, the way she flossed three times a day. *Something.*"

His description of Nicole was right on the mark. But anyone meticulous enough to dig up George Abbot's name could dig up all these things as well. On the other hand, she realized she was beginning to give up. If he wasn't William Chastain, who was he and what did he want with her?

"Okay, I'll play along," she said, searching her memory for some obscure detail of Nicole's life. "I know. Tell me what kind of diet she started after Christmas."

He looked startled by her question. "I was living on my boat by then. I saw her when I came to see Leo and she did as much to make that next to impossible as she could.

"Besides, she was always on a diet. Wait, we met for lunch in January. She complained she'd gained half a pound over the holidays. Half a pound. I didn't even know they made home scales that measured down to half a pound. Let's see. She settled on some kind of seaweed algae smoothie. It looked like bilgewater. Smelled like it, too."

"It did smell like bilgewater," Julia said.

"Well?"

"You're William Chastain?"

"Call me Will. Only Nicole insisted on calling me William."

"Nicole told me a lot…well, about you."

"None of it good, right?"

"No, not much."

His voice softened. "Things were good at the beginning, but you didn't know her then. By the time you discovered she existed, things had gone sour. My fault as much as hers."

It was decision time. Julia, trusting her gut instinct, said, "Okay."

"Does that mean you'll take me along?"

"Yes. But I'm warning you, I know how to defend myself."

This time his smile reached his eyes. "I don't doubt it for a minute," he said.

WILL CLOSED his eyes. He couldn't remember the last time he'd slept without visions of exploding boats tearing him from sleep. Days, maybe. His eyes felt gritty, as though he'd been caught in a sandstorm. His arm throbbed where the car had thumped him. His hip no doubt sported a black-and-blue mark the size of a salad plate.

And he was hungry. For the first time in days, he was hungry.

"When's the last time you saw Nicole?" he asked. They were just exiting the freeway, Julia driving fast. He found her impatience reassuring.

She didn't answer.

He'd been thinking about Julia ever since he'd learned his child was to be given to her, handed over by Nicole's directive. He'd tried to recall what Nicole had said about her cousin. "Mousy and shy" were the terms

Nicole had most often used when describing Julia.

He sneaked a look at Julia's profile. No, she wasn't flashy like Nicole. It didn't look as though she spent a lot of time pouting or posturing, either. She came across as a loner. From the first moment he'd spied her in the airport, he'd recognized in her the same aura of isolation he carried inside himself.

Mousy? No. Her brown hair was windblown but luxuriant, her dark eyes intelligent, her tall frame athletic but curvy. She wore her blue jeans like a second skin, and the suppleness of the sable leather jacket set off her hair and eyes while mimicking the smooth texture of her skin.

His hand drifted to the bandage on his arm—her white scarf—ruined now by his blood. Well, no wonder Nicole wrote her cousin off as little more than a babysitter for those times when Leo became an inconvenience. His wife had been a tad egotistical. She seldom picked up on nuances, either, and wouldn't have differentiated shyness from restraint.

"Two weeks before you were reported dead," Julia said.

It took him a second to realize she was answering his question.

"Nicole called to ask me if she could leave Leo with me for a weekend. But I was working and I said no."

Her voice choked up on the last word. He was beginning to understand that Leo's plight was personal to her. He hadn't understood how close she'd become to his son.

Okay. Nicole had wanted a weekend free. Out of town, out of state, for that matter. A lover's tryst with a man whose face and position were too well known to stay close to home while romancing a woman other than his wife? Would Nicole's chief of police boyfriend come along or would they have met somewhere? He said, "Did she ever bring any friends to your house when she brought Leo over?"

"Friends?"

"Men," he said.

She darted him a glance and then turned her concentration back to the road. "No," she said.

"Does it surprise you to hear she had a boyfriend?"

"No," she said, not looking at him this time. "Tell me why you pretended you were dead and why you let Leo leave Washington."

He had known this was coming. He'd prepared a few lies. But now, sitting in the dark car, too tired to dissimilate, he chose the truth. "I'm pretty sure Nicole set up my supposed accident. I got a call from a woman claiming to have compromising pictures of my wife and her husband. She said she'd hired a private eye to get them. Told me they were mine for the taking."

"Why didn't the woman use them herself?"

"She said she was afraid of her husband. Claimed he was the chief of police. She told me to meet her at a restaurant across the river. The fastest way there was on my boat so I took it. Only someone who knew me well would know that's what I would do."

"Nicole, for instance."

"Of the people interested in our small world of problems, only Nicole. Anyway, I was living on the boat by then so all my papers, everything I valued besides my son, were aboard."

"And it exploded?"

"It was hit by another boat going like a bat out of hell. I got off in the nick of time.

The newspaper the next day said that human remains were found were are being tested for DNA to see which boater they belong to, me or the nameless other guy. Contrary to what television leads us to believe, the testing can take a while. A small speedboat was reported stolen from a nearby marina. Recovered wreckage confirmed that it was the boat that hit mine."

"But you don't think it was an accident?"

"No."

"Why?"

He thought for a moment. "It came right at me. I turned on every light and still it came. The next day I called the chief of police's house. A servant informed me that the chief's wife was in the hospital following childbirth complications. Had been for several days. Hard to picture her calling me from a hospital bed, then sneaking out to rendezvous at a restaurant across the river. I don't doubt the affair. I just doubt the pictures and the setup."

"So you determined Nicole must have been behind it?"

"Who else? I didn't want her or the boyfriend to know they weren't successful. A man in that position has serious clout. I'm just an architect, a relative unknown. I thought if I was declared dead, I could uncover some kind of evidence that would prove Nicole and her lover guilty of attempted murder. Then I could use that proof to gain custody of Leo."

"But before all that could happen, Nicole drove off the side of the highway and crashed into a tree."

"Yes. With Leo in the car. It's a miracle he wasn't hurt. By the time I found out she was dead, Leo was in protective custody. How could I prove who I was without sounding like a nutcase? How could I tell the authorities my story, including the chief's part in it without endangering my chances of ever recovering my boy?

"In the end, I decided it would be best to let Leo come to you. It would give me time to reestablish my identity before approaching you. But I had to make sure he got here safe and sound and that you were…capable…of watching him." He paused for a second. The truth was that he'd been afraid Julia was a carbon copy of Nicole. He'd had to make sure she was willing to take on a child for even a few weeks, as well as be responsible enough not to do him harm. He added, "I thought if you were halfway reasonable, I could talk to you about this and we could work something out."

His voice trailed off. He didn't know what else to say. Everything so far made him sound like an idiot.

"That's why you were at the airport? Just to watch me take custody of Leo?"

"Yes."

Her voice took on an impatient tone as she added, "Then did you see the imposter? The woman pretending to be me? A tall man in a gray raincoat?"

He shook his head. "I was late. I got there after you. I recognized Nicole's lawyer so I had to stay out of his line of vision. The panic on your face when you turned to catch me staring at you just about tore my gut open."

She cast him a quick glance. Even in the dim light, he caught the sparkle in her eyes that suggested pooling tears.

Julia's hand strayed to her face where he presumed she brushed away the tears. Damn, her raw emotions touched him more than he liked. She was a grown-up. Her past and her problems were not his concern.

"Where do you think Leo is?" she asked at last.

"I think he's with my aunt," he said.

This earned him a longer glance, which she jerked away only because she needed to watch the road. As she guided the car around a corner, she almost whispered, "Why would your aunt steal your son in such an elaborate ruse?"

"Fiona Chastain is sophisticated and wealthy and she hated Nicole's guts. The feeling was mutual."

"So that's why I was chosen as guardian and not your aunt."

"I can't imagine the words the two of them must have exchanged after my supposed death. I'm betting Aunt Fiona caught wind of Nicole's decision to provide for Leo in the event of her death and over-reacted. She's got lots of connections. I think she put this elaborate hoax into operation as soon as she learned she'd been bypassed as Leo's guardian. I checked the airline schedules. There was a flight leaving for Spokane just minutes after you think you spotted Leo and his abductors in the elevator. My aunt happens to have relocated to Spokane."

"But I would have been happy to share

Leo with your aunt," Julia said. "I would have loved knowing he had more family—"

"My aunt wouldn't see things that way," he said. Picking the next words with care, he added, "She's very…controlling."

"What did you mean that he was in no danger except for disappearing?"

"Fiona has the means and knowledge to disappear at will. If she goes underground with Leo, I don't know how I'll ever find him again."

He could tell she thought he was overstating things. He didn't blame her. He added, "I know this, Julia, because that's how she raised me."

"Moving you, hiding you—"

"Yes."

"Nicole told me you were orphaned."

"Father disappeared before birth, identity and location unknown. Mom died after giving birth. Her sister, Aunt Fiona, stepped in and took me. She was a fierce parent."

"Who would never hurt you."

"She thinks I'm dead, remember? I should have contacted her, but I didn't trust her not to say something to Nicole. In retrospect, it was cruel on my part to do this to her."

"Then the thing in the parking garage,"

Julia said, her glance taking in his bandaged arm this time, "had to be an accident."

"No. I don't think so. I don't know what that was about, but there was a calculated air about the whole thing. It wasn't until the car revved up and headed straight for you that I realized I'd been aware of an idling engine for some time."

"Just a moment. Your aunt tried to run me down?"

"No, of course not. That's what I mean about things not making sense."

"You can say that again," she said, making another turn.

"Fiona wouldn't have done any of this herself. She would have arranged it. Maybe one of her minions got creative."

This remark was met with silence.

"It's at least a place to start," he said as they turned yet another corner. Though it had stopped raining and a full moon bathed the streets, he knew he'd never find his way out of this maze of streets and look-alike houses without help. He pushed aside the thought of leaving. First he had to make sure Julia's house was safe for her to return to, and then he'd contact his aunt and figure out transportation—

She said, "The police—"

"The police aren't going to be able to solve this situation," he said. "They'll wait for a ransom call that will never come. They'll appeal to the public. My son's photo will end up on a milk carton if they still do that. If I want Leo back, I'm going to have to get him myself."

As she made another turn, her voice turned thoughtful. "I'm going to go about this the traditional way," she said. "I'm going to rely on the cops and wait for a call. I can't take the chance that I'll let Leo down again, that I won't be there when the right time occurs."

He sneaked another look at her. Was it possible she'd forgotten that Leo no longer needed her as a guardian, at least for the long term, that his father was alive and well and sitting in the seat next to her?

Or did she still not believe he was who he said he was?

Or maybe she'd just written him off. God Almighty, she wouldn't try to take Leo away from him, would she? Claim he was unbalanced or that his wacky aunt had undue influence?

That aunt of his. She'd been his salvation

and his cross to bear, as touchy as a rattle-snake, as crafty as a third-world despot.

Irritated with Julia's obstinacy, he looked out the window. The neighborhood through which they traveled wasn't ritzy. Lawns looked sparse. The moonlight revealed too many abandoned toys littering driveways and front yards. Lots of cars, most older than the compact in which he rode, which had to be entering its teens. Compared to the lakeside community he'd been working on before his supposed death, this place looked like a slum. Even his and Nicole's high-rise condo looked classy in comparison. It was hard to picture Nicole even visiting such modest surroundings.

But more to the point, how could Julia believe anyone would stage such an intricate kidnapping to gain custody of Leo just to ransom him back to a woman who drove an old car and lived in a very modest house? The certainty his aunt was behind this doubled.

Julia pulled her aging sedan into the driveway of a small square house. The wash of headlights revealed well-tended plants and no accumulated junk. Other than that, it looked very much like every other house on the block.

"Home," she said with a touch of anxiety he realized he'd planted. She was nervous. Good. Might keep her on her toes.

Okay, he shouldn't have accompanied Julia home. Now he was stuck out here with a phone tapped by the police. But he couldn't let her return to a house that could be booby-trapped when she wouldn't be in this mess if it weren't for him. He'd check out the house, figure out his next step, warn her about locking up and disappear into the night.

Easier said than done, but he'd do it just the same. The most important thing was to get Leo back.

Clothes and ID weren't the only things he'd lost when his boat exploded. Also gone were his laptop, cell phone and address book, all of which held his aunt's unlisted number. He'd never bothered to memorize her number. Why bother when it was always handy? A man doesn't expect to have his whole life blown apart.

"Do you have a computer?" he asked.

"Yes."

She was soon out of the car, pulling the blue stuffed animal from the back where he'd tossed it when he got in the passenger seat. Maybe he could use her computer to access the address book on his computer at work. Of course, since the architectural firm of Wainwright and Co. thought he was dead, they may well have terminated his access... He'd have to see.

And he'd also have to talk Julia Sheridan out of her car.

Reenergized with a plan of action, he got out of the car and followed Julia up the front walk toward her door. She should have left lights burning for her return, but then he recalled she hadn't expected to get back after dark.

He was about to step in front of her when he noticed a faint line of light stripping the long vertical edge of the door. He glanced to his left, through what appeared to be her kitchen window.

He pulled Julia back against his chest, moving backward.

"Hey—" she gasped before he slapped a hand over her mouth. Loosening his grip, he leaned forward until his lips brushed her ear. "Your front door is ajar. There's a light bobbing around in there," he whispered. "Someone with a flashlight."

To his absolute amazement, she tore

herself free and stormed toward her unlocked door, ripping it open and charging inside before he could stop her.

Raised voices reached him as he crossed the threshold in her wake.

A moment later, a gunshot thundered through the house.

Chapter Three

As the dark shape of a man charged toward her, Julia swung Leo's stuffed elephant by its trunk. She felt the impact as she hit something. A male voice swore. She kicked what she hoped was a leg, kicked hard, aiming for the side of the kneecap where it would do the most damage. If she connected.

She hit something. Her foot throbbed as a gun fired and someone ran over the top of her.

"Get off me!" she screamed, kicking and throwing punches, driven now by fear as well as anger.

Will's voice reached her. "Are you hurt?" he yelled, all but lifting her to her feet.

"Get him!" she cried, pointing at the sliding glass door that led to the backyard where the dark figure of her attacker, highlighted against the light coming through the glass, struggled with the latch.

Will darted toward the door. Julia heard it slide open and the dark shape disappeared into her yard, Will on his heels.

She staggered to the door, flipping on the yard light just in time to see Will leap over the low fence in the back, still in pursuit. Both men disappeared into the merciless shadows of the neighbor's yard.

She found other light switches and flipped them all on, illuminating every dark corner.

The gunshot had taken off a corner of a plaster wall and shattered a mirror. But not before it had torn through the elephant, almost severing its neck, ripping its blue fur, blasting out an eyeball. Stuffing, piled like snow drifts, littered the floor along with shards of glass from the mirror. Julia dropped the elephant—it was beyond saving. She swept the glass and stuffing against the floorboards where it wouldn't be a hazard.

She would have to get Leo a new stuffed animal. The thought brought more tears to her eyes.

Moving from room to room, she found a pillow case missing from one of the pillows on her bed. Besides that, only a couple of open drawers drew her attention until it dawned on her that the few nice things she owned were gone.

A locket belonging to her mother. A silver frame around a picture of her sister. Her father's modest coin collection. Her whole family, gone, and now the precious few mementoes she'd managed to hold on to after years of turmoil gone as well.

As were a few pieces of costume jewelry and the silver-plated ladle she'd received as a Christmas gift. From Nicole.

Julia picked up the cordless phone to call 911. She paused on the last digit, clicking the phone off, resettling it on the charger base, glancing toward the door through which Will had disappeared.

What in the hell was going on?

What kind of burglar robs a house in a neighborhood like this one, settling on a few ornaments when the computer and stereo were worth far more?

"Tweakers," her boss, George Abbot, called them. His brother was a cop and George enjoyed throwing out the lingo. He was referring to meth addicts, people who stole just to finance their next high. Petty crime, as a rule of thumb, nonviolent. That kind of break-in was common around here.

But the gun—

Julia plopped down on the inexpensive overstuffed red chair she'd bought on deferred payments just hours before news of Nicole's death had reached her. Stilling her trembling hands by sitting on them, she looked at the few other pieces of furniture, each chosen to complement the sunny-yellow paint of the walls.

This house was her castle. In daylight, sun streamed through the windows and pooled on the floors. After dark, it became a sanctuary, a place in which to retreat from the world. It was the reason she'd marched through the front door without thinking and almost gotten herself shot dead.

She'd left that morning intending to share her home with a tiny boy who needed her. She'd come home empty-handed, the child's whereabouts unknown, his future in jeopardy, her haven violated.

And now his father was here, a dead man, only not dead. Where was Will?

When the phone rang, Julia popped to her feet. Her heart rate doubled. The kidnappers! It had to be.

"Hello?" she said, listening for some sound, a clicking, a whir, that would indicate the police had activated the tracing device. Of course, advanced technology no doubt precluded telltale sounds—

"Miss Sheridan? This is Detective Morris."

Taking a deep breath, she said, "Detective Morris."

"Sorry to alarm you," he said. "Just calling to see if you made it home okay."

"Well—"

"I want you to know we'll have a police car patrolling your neighborhood tonight, starting at midnight. There are no new developments at the airport. Any word from the kidnappers? Any new developments we should know about?"

She should tell him about her intruder…

Her gaze strayed to the glass door as Will Chastain made his way across her well-lit patio, a bag of some kind dangling from his right hand. Relieved to see him still in one piece, she took a deep breath. He looked up and their eyes met.

She said, "Nothing to report, Detective."

"You're sure?"

"Yes. Did Monsieur Pepin return to Washington?"

"We let him go a couple of hours ago. We know where to find him. He was very upset. He feels responsible."

Don't we all? Julia thought.

"You call if you need anything. We'll monitor all your incoming calls."

"I understand," she said, replacing the receiver as Will let himself in the sliding glass door.

"He got away," he said, crossing the floor in his socks. He pointed at the phone and added, "You called the cops?"

"No. They called me." As a flicker of hope ignited his eyes, she added, "It was a routine call, nothing more."

"I see. Did you tell them about…this?"

Her knees wobbled. Julia sat down again. Some of it was the culmination of the day's events, some of it was the profound relief that Will had returned unharmed.

If he *was* Will Chastain. But even that automatic mental disqualifier felt feeble now. She'd started accepting him as who he said he was some time before. For better or worse, she'd bought into his story.

And now she coveted his presence. Disheveled and weathered though he was, he exuded confidence and something more.

Determination. That was it. Nothing was going to stop him. No one was going to keep him from Leo. What must it be like to be loved like that, wanted like that? It struck her that if Leo was ever going to return to her—to them—Will was going to have to be a part of it. And she wanted to be a part of it, too.

She said, "I didn't mention any of…this."

"Because?"

"I guess I thought we should talk about it first," she said.

"Then let's talk."

"First tell me what happened out there," she said, gesturing at the only other chair in the room. It was orange and armless, not really comfortable, chosen for its color and price tag rather than its function. That had seemed the way to decorate to Julia who, before decorating this house, had never even chosen a bedspread for herself.

He brought her the sack which she'd more or less forgotten about until he placed it in her hands. It was the pillowcase off her bed, a fact she'd registered when he'd come through the door with it dangling from his hand. In it, she found all her missing items.

Trinkets. Mementoes of a scratchy past, of people whose faces had faded in her mind.

Studying the bullet-sheared wall and the mess of stuffing and plaster and glass swept against the baseboard, Will whistled. "Thank the Lord our thief is a lousy shot or you'd be dead," he said as he perched on the edge of the orange chair. There were bright smears of blood on the scarf still wrapped around his arm. There were also new streaks of mud on his pants and caked on his shoes. He looked absolutely exhausted.

At first Nicole had often commented on her husband's good looks and his success as an architect. The comments had morphed, though, into how cruel he was. No specifics, just words like *selfish* and *callous* which Julia had always understood to mean he wasn't giving Nicole everything she wanted.

He said, "I chased him through at least five backyards. Woke up every dog in the neighborhood. The guy had a limp, but he ran like hell. I think I would have caught him except that I slipped in some mud and he scampered over another fence. I heard a car door, but by the time I got to the fence and looked over, he was peeling away from the curb."

Julia, proud that her kick had connected with the intruder's leg, said, "Was the car the same—"

"As the one from the parking garage? I don't know. It could have been. Same low profile, same general color but other than that…I just don't know."

"It has to be connected," Julia said.

"Explain."

"Well, just that so many odd and terrible things have happened today. First the blowout on the freeway—"

He sat forward, hands gripped together between his knees, eyes burning. "Yes. Tell me about that."

She shrugged. "What's to tell? The tire blew."

"How fast were you driving?"

"Well, the freeway was crowded. I'd just slowed down to about fifty when the right front tire blew."

"Which lane were you in?"

"Far left. It was hairy for a few minutes but I managed to get the car across three lanes to the shoulder. I was kind of shaken up. A guy behind me stopped. He insisted on taking off the old tire and putting on the spare. He wasn't very proficient. And he was dressed in a suit. The drizzle made it nasty out there and I let him help me."

"It strikes me that you're the kind of woman who changes her own tire," Will said.

"Yes," she said. She thought for a moment. "He was so insistent," she said. "He had an accent I couldn't place. I thought maybe it was a matter of honor for him. I asked him where he was from, but he didn't seem to understand me. In the end it was just easier…or so I thought at first…but he was an absolute klutz and I was late and then Leo was gone—"

He was at her side. Taking her hands, he pulled her to her feet and wrapped his arms around her. She hadn't known she was shaking until she felt his warm, solid embrace.

It was tempting to lean, tempting to give him her burdens. Tempting to depend on him. Taking a step away, she took a deep breath and did none of those things.

"What did the guy on the freeway look like?"

Biting her lip in concentration, she forced his image into her mind. "Medium build. Dark hair and eyes. A little bit of a tan which

I noticed because you don't see that very often in San Francisco in April. Dark suit." She shrugged and added, "Kind of average."

"Sounds pretty much like the guy who shot at you just now, doesn't it?"

She nodded. It could have been the same man. Of course, her description was so vague it could have fit lots of people. Besides, it was dark and her shooter hadn't spoken this time. She'd made all the racket.

"Show me your flat tire," Will said.

She started to ask why and let it go. She couldn't see what the tire would tell him, but she was beginning to trust his instincts. Taking a flashlight off the kitchen counter, she took him through the empty garage to the driveway where she'd parked the car and opened the trunk. Will took the flashlight from her and examined the tire. She'd been in such a hurry that she'd just thrown it in without cinching it down. The panic of the moments when she realized she was going to be late picking up Leo at the airport came rushing back.

"Look," Will said, focusing the light on the tire. "See this hole? That's the entry wound, so to speak. The shredded rubber on the opposite side is where it exited. If the traffic hadn't slowed…if you'd been racing along at seventy you would have lost control for sure."

She stared at the hole, refusing to believe what her eyes told her.

"Someone shot your tire," he said.

The concrete beneath Julia's feet seemed to rumble.

"That's why the guy who stopped behind you didn't want you fooling with the tire," Will added. "You weren't supposed to survive this attack."

"But he must have known I'd see the tire later—"

"You're forgetting the attempt to run you down in the parking garage and then the 'burglar' in your house, lying in wait for you with a gun—the tire would have disappeared, Julia."

She stared at the hole, jumping when Will slammed the trunk. Looking up and down the empty street, he took her arm. "Go back in the house, please," he said, his voice little more than a whisper. "First, leave me your keys so I can move the car into the garage. Lock all the doors. I'll be in right after you."

She did as he asked without argument.

An entry wound, Will had called it.

A place where a bullet had pierced the tire before exploding out the other side. Shot with the hope that the car would pile into others, causing a catastrophic wreck, killing who knew how many people. Killing her.

What in the world was going on?

A SLY SMILE played across Will's lips as his attempt to hack into the company's computer system went through without a hitch. He knew he owed his luck to Brian Wainwright's tendency to procrastinate, a tendency that had driven Will crazy for years.

But not tonight.

"Thanks, Brian, you lazy SOB," he whispered.

As he printed out his address book, he caught the sound of the running shower. Despite the late hour—it was closing in on midnight—Julia had announced her decision to bathe with a defiant look on her pretty face. He wasn't sure to what he should attribute that look. His presence in her home? The intruder, the attempts on her life, the kidnapping of Leo?

The woman had had quite a day.

And she was taking him on faith. Worrisome.

He'd refused her attempts to bathe and bandage his arm. He couldn't afford the time. It seemed as though they were standing still, that Leo was moving farther and farther away.

But he hadn't refused the offer of a ham sandwich and a glass of milk. After polishing off the last of both, he unwound Julia's white wool scarf from his arm, glancing around what was to have been his son's room. Julia hadn't gotten too far on the decorating. Blue walls, a blue synthetic oriental-type rug, one side of the room taken up with a single bed, a desk and the computer equipment. A box against the other wall held a crib yet to be assembled. Another box held a high chair. She'd cleared off the top of a dresser and stacked disposable diapers and baby-related items like baby oil and wiping cloths, a brand-new package of pacifiers, bibs, swabs.

It jarred him to think that these things were meant for *his* son.

He dumped the scarf in the garbage. The bleeding had stopped. Of course, the sleeve of the suit and the shirt beneath were torn and stained. Along with his muddy pants and wacky hair, he must present quite an attractive package.

She walked into the room just as he lifted the paper from her printer.

"Did you find your aunt's phone number?"

"Yes," he said, turning to face her. No femme fatale outfit for Julia Sheridan, he saw. She had changed into gray sweatpants and a pink T-shirt, both on the baggy side. Her brown hair was wet and shiny, caught in a ponytail, her skin rosy. She looked sixteen. Way too young and innocent to be in the same room with him.

She handed him the phone, but he shook his head. "I don't want the cops listening in," he said as he folded the pages and stuck them in a pocket. "May I use your cell phone?"

She left the room without comment and he followed her into the kitchen. She'd started a pot of coffee and he poured himself a cup as she dug her cell phone from her handbag.

His aunt didn't answer. He left a phone number but not his name. In fact, he didn't identify himself at all, just urged her to return his call at the first opportunity, day or night.

"Does she have a cell phone? Is there another number you could call?"

"She has one but she doesn't leave it on. Uses it to make calls but hates being a 'slave' to it. Besides, odds are at this time of the night she was there, listening to my message."

"Why wouldn't she answer you?"

"You're forgetting the last news she had about me was that I perished in a boating accident. Even if she hears this message, she'll be wary that it's me. If she doesn't call soon, I'll call her back."

They stood staring at each other for several moments as Will sipped the coffee without tasting it. It came to him that he was beginning to think of Julia as a woman, not just as Nicole's little cousin or Leo's surrogate mother. He was beginning to notice the shape of her body, the thrust of her breasts against her T-shirt, the softness of her lips in repose, the expressions that flashed across her face at breakneck speed.

He wanted to know more about her.

But first he wanted sleep. And a shower and clean clothes. And most of all, Leo safe in his arms.

She said, "I think you'd better start wondering who else would steal your son, Will. And I'd better start wondering who wants me dead."

Will couldn't answer either question, though he wondered if his past, swathed in a suffocating silence his aunt had always refused to break, could have played a part in Leo's abduction. He couldn't picture anyone wanting to kill Julia unless it was connected to Leo's disappearance. Someone was afraid she could identify them. That's what made sense.

A banging on the front door interrupted the silence that had descended after Julia's last observations. A male voice called, "Julia? Julia, are you in there? Open up!"

"It's a little late for callers," Will said, glancing at the flower wall clock. It was after midnight now. He set aside his coffee mug.

"I forgot all about George," she said, hurrying to answer the door. By the time Will rounded the corner, he found Julia engulfed in a tall man's arms. She burst into tears.

Who the hell was George?

"I MEANT TO CALL you," Julia said when she came up for air. Embarrassed by her tears and the emotional meltdown that had prompted them, she kept her gaze fastened on a wall somewhere between the two men.

By then, George had steered her into the living room and Will had closed and locked the front door. "I kind of forgot," she added.

"Damn it, Julia, what's going on here?" George demanded. Nearing forty, George Abbot was not only Julia's boss at Abbot Air Transport, but also her friend. They'd tried dating a while ago. They'd tried hard. But George had pointed out that anything special between a man and a woman shouldn't take so much effort and they'd gone back to being friends. It had been a profound relief to Julia, who had to admit to herself that what George represented to her was a father figure, not a lover.

"Did the police—"

"Grill me like I was a common criminal? Yes, they did," George said. "Who would impersonate me and pretend to be your fiancé? Where'd they get that? I think the cops are still watching me. There's a patrol car in your neighborhood. I passed it coming in—"

"They're just watching the house. It has nothing to do with you. I'm sorry I didn't warn you—"

"Seems like you've been busy," George said with a glance at Will.

"It's been quite a night," she agreed. Would Will introduce himself to George? And if he did, would they then have to try to explain how he got here, why he wasn't dead? Would George feel honor-bound to tell the police—

"Good thing I had an alibi," George added. "Been with Barbara all day. Her and her girls. Amber is on a basketball team. Tournament today. Just got home a little while ago and there were the cops, waiting for me."

Julia refrained from apologizing again. George was perturbed. She didn't blame him. Barbara was the new love of his life and he was crazy about her preteen daughters as well. It must have ruined his day to come home after a fun time of games and laughter to antagonistic questioning.

"Guess the important thing now is to find your cousin's baby," he said, some of his bluster dissipating. He was still eyeing Will with suspicion. He said, "You a cop?"

Julia didn't see how anyone as savvy as George about police matters could mistake Will in his present condition for a cop.

You thought he was airport security, a little

voice in her head whispered. *Sometimes a person sees what they expect to see—*

Will said, "Something like that. I'm here to help Julia."

George's nod was brisk. It looked as though the matter of Will's identity was settled in his mind.

"I think I should try making that call," Will added.   "The phone is on the counter."

She listened to George describe his police interrogation with half an ear. With the other half, she listened as Will placed his call. When it was obvious he was speaking to someone, she stilled George with a hand and hurried to Will's side.

"Honest, Aunt Fiona, it *is* me," he was saying as his gaze met Julia's. He turned the corner in the kitchen, placing himself out of view of the living room, sandwiching himself between the refrigerator and the sink. Julia followed. Lowering his voice, he said into the phone, "It was a terrible thing for me to do to you and I'm sorry. I'll explain very soon, I promise. But right now I need to know if you have Leo."

He listened for just a moment, his forehead wrinkling. "Why are you being so evasive?" he asked.

After a pause, he said, "I'd understand if you thought you should rescue him from Nicole's relatives." With this he glanced at Julia and shrugged. "What I mean is that you thought I was dead. I know you would want to protect the little guy."

He listened for a few more seconds before switching to a calming voice. "I get the feeling you can't talk right now. Are you okay?"

After a brief pause, he said, "I understand." She must have reassured him though his expression didn't look reassured. He added, "I'll come see you soon—"

Now his eyes narrowed and his mouth formed a straight line. He said, "Polo," waiting with what seemed suspended breath before snapping, "Fiona? Aunt Fiona?"

He folded Julia's phone and looked at her. "Something is wrong," he said.

"What do you mean, wrong?"

For the first time, Julia was aware that George had joined them in the kitchen and stood with his hands behind his back, listening.

Will seemed too distracted to notice or care. He said, "It's a code she taught me eons ago. Nothing unique. She uses the name

Marco in a sentence. I answer with Polo to let her know I'm on to her. We used to joke that if either one of us ever made a friend named Marco we'd have to come up with a new code."

"What does the code mean?" George asked.

Will's head snapped up and he met George's gaze. "It means to stay away, that she'll contact me when it's safe." Looking at Julia, he added, "Back when I was a kid, I knew it meant not to go home. To stay where I was until she came for me. Soon afterwards, I'd have a new name, a new house, a new school."

"This is part of that odd upbringing you mentioned," Julia said.

"Yes."

Julia's cell phone erupted. Will was still holding it. He flipped it open and glanced at the screen. "My aunt's calling back," he said, followed by a tap of a button and a soft, "Yes?" into the phone.

He listened for a moment before snapping, "Who's this?" He lowered the phone, once again clicking it shut.

"Whoever it was hung up without identifying themselves."

"It wasn't your aunt?"

"Why would she have called without speaking? It was her number, but it was someone else on the phone. Someone was with her, I'm sure of it. She must have caller ID now. When she refused to tell them who it was, they called to check for themselves. I have to get back to Washington."

He pushed the phone into Julia's hands.

"But your aunt's code to stay where you are—"

"I'm not a child anymore," he said. "I don't stay when I'm told to. I have an awful feeling she's in jeopardy and that it's tied to Leo."

"What about calling the police where she is? Someone might be able to go check—"

"No. You don't know my aunt. No cops. I have to go."

She caught his arm. "You can't walk, Will. I'll drive you back to the airport."

He looked self-conscious as he said, "A ride to the interstate will suffice."

Of course. He didn't have any money. How could she have overlooked something as familiar as being broke?

"You can take my car," she said, digging in her purse for a credit card that wasn't up to its limit. "Use this for gas money. I can't leave here and go with you. If the kidnappers call I have to be here."

"They won't call," Will insisted. "Don't you understand? This is tied up with my aunt, maybe back to my deep dark past, hell, I don't know. But it isn't some garden-variety kidnapper wanting a few bucks. You need to go somewhere safe. To a motel or something." Pausing a second he added, "Or come with me."

She wanted to go. The intensity of that want all but drowned her. Yet how did she abandon her post? She knew Leo's best chance was his father. No one loved him as much, no one needed him as much—

Except her.

They'd both forgotten about George again. He shifted his weight and brought his hands from behind his back. He held what was left of the blue elephant.

"You're not a cop, are you?" he said.

Will swore before grumbling, "This is not my day for fooling anyone."

"You're connected to the little boy?"

"He's my son."

"Julia thought you were dead."

"I know. I don't have to time to explain—"

George held up both hands, the elephant dangling, bleeding stuffing. "Hell, I don't want an explanation. Even I can see something terrible is going on here." Reaching in his pocket, he extracted a ring of keys and took one off. "Take my truck, the both of you. I'll stay here. Take your cell phone, Julia, and I'll let you know when and if a ransom call comes."

"George, I can't—"

"Your car won't make it to Washington, we both know that. Wait, I have a better idea. Drive the truck to the field and take the Skyhawk. It's all fueled up and ready to go."

"That's your personal plane, George. It's brand-new. I couldn't—"

"You'll have it back before I can miss it," he said. "Besides, all the others are tied up with business tomorrow. Go ahead, take it. You'll be there in a few hours that way."

Now Will protested. "You don't know a thing about me."

"No. But I do know Julia. And I trust her. Judging from the bullet lodged in the molding in the living room, she's in danger. So are your aunt and your kid. Look, I don't want to lose my best pilot." His gaze lingering on Will's torn, bloodied sleeve, he added,

"When you get to my office, take a few minutes and go upstairs. There's a shower up there and clean clothes. We're about the same size, help yourself to what you need."

"I'll repay you," Will said. "When I get my life back. When I find my son—"

"Good. Fuel's expensive. Just take care of Julia."

"You can count on it."

"We can take my car—" Julia began, but Will stilled her with a glance. "You don't have a spare. We can't chance getting stuck out on the road. Take George's truck. Leave his key on his desk. Let's go."

The two men shook hands. Their pact seemed to relegate Julia to the role of damsel in distress. A flicker of annoyance fizzled in a cold wave of rational thought. Face it, they were more or less right about her. Someone was trying to kill her and she didn't have the faintest idea how to protect herself. From a mugger? Sure. But from a gun, fired from far away or a car aimed at her in an intersection? No way.

Besides, the look in Will's eyes was anything but boastful. He looked as though he was holding himself together by sheer force of will.

Julia hugged George. "The police are going to think I flipped my lid," Julia muttered. "I haven't told them about a lot of this. They don't know about Will, for instance."

George waggled the pathetic remains of the elephant. "Or what happened here, right? Don't worry. I'll tell them there was an emergency and you took off. I imagine they'll figure out you're on the trail of the kidnappers, though, so you'd better get a head start."

"Thanks, George. Oh, call Mrs. Landers in the morning, will you? She's supposed to babysit Leo. And Maria and Janet from the office were going to come over tomorrow night to meet Leo—will you call them, too?"

"I'll take care of things. Now, go," George said.

"And you be careful," she added.

After changing clothes, she packed a few essentials into the even roomier shoulder bag she used when traveling. They left the house together, calling goodbye to George who had settled into the red chair. Julia glanced back at her small oasis once before turning the first corner.

Would she ever see home again?

Chapter Four

Will closed his eyes as he stood under George Abbot's shower, hoping the hot spray would clear his head, knowing it was going to take several solid hours of sleep to accomplish such a thing. A clear head was going to have to wait.

The burning question was easy: Despite what his aunt said, did she have Leo? Had some crazy scheme to take him backfired into this current mess? Who was with her and why had she passed on the Marco Polo code? And the real underlying terror: if she didn't have Leo, if she was not involved in his abduction, who was? Where in God's name was his baby?

Wincing when he lifted his left arm, he peered down to study the scratches and scrapes on his bicep. The car bumper or license plate must have nicked him. The abrasion had started bleeding again and a bluish cast to the surrounding skin suggested a bruise in the making. His hip sported similar telltale signs of bruising. He lathered his arm and rinsed it, working his muscles, knowing he might need them a few hours from now. He couldn't afford to freeze up.

He found Julia standing outside the shower, eyes closed, towel in her hand. She'd changed into a light blue jumpsuit with Abbot Air Transport embroidered on the breast pocket in red thread. The outfit became her, emphasizing her tall, curvy figure, her small waist. The color of the jumpsuit set off the deep-brown luster of her hair, still pulled back in a ponytail, this time looped through the closure in the back of a matching baseball cap.

"What are you doing in here?" he said as he took the towel and wrapped it around his waist. "You can open your eyes now."

She did, and the deep brown irises looked a trifle uneasy as though she wasn't accustomed to standing so near nude strangers. After so many years around Nicole, who seldom if ever showed the least touch of inhibition, he found Julia's reticence kind of sweet.

She nodded at the first aid kit she'd deposited on the small drain board. "I thought you might need help bandaging your arm," she said, dabbing at the bright red streaks of blood running down his arm with a clean wad of gauze. "Sit down," she told him.

He was too tired to argue. There was only one place to perch in the room, the toilet seat. "Just make it quick," he said, his voice gruff.

"I also need to know where we're going so I can file a flight plan."

"My aunt lives in Spokane, Washington."

"Good enough." She applied antibacterial cream, then wrapped a thick bandage around his arm with long strips of gauze. He looked up at her as she worked. Her gaze was steady, her lashes long and thick, her cheeks flushed pink, her lips pursed. A sudden impulse to pull her down onto his lap just about made him fall to the floor.

He must have jerked for she stopped bandaging and looked into his eyes. "Did I hurt you?"

He fought the urge to reach up, cup her chin, run his fingers across her cheek and coax her mouth down to his level. Her gaze softened as though she knew what he was thinking and wouldn't stop him if he tried.

"That's enough bandaging. We don't have time for this. Get out of here so I can get dressed."

"But I'm not finished—"

"Please."

"I'll go finish the preflight check-in," she told him.

"Good. Just hurry." His voice sounded curt. Curt wasn't what he wanted, but what he wanted didn't matter. Julia was an exquisite, caring woman who was beginning to look at him in that way a woman does when her interest is piqued. It was the same way he was looking at her. Their timing was lousy, but it wasn't her fault. He added, "Thanks. For everything."

She met his gaze once again before lowering hers and, gathering her supplies together, she left without another word.

He dressed in blue jeans only a little too big and a dark blue sweatshirt. He put back on the loafers in which he'd chased the intruder. Wadding up the torn, ill-fitting suit, he deposited it in the garbage can. The mirror reflected a man who could use a shave, but there was no time for that. A jacket with the Abbot Air Transport logo went on over the sweatshirt as he hurried down the stairs.

He'd found Abbot Air to be a modest-looking operation located at a small airport right outside Madrone. Julia had explained the Fixed Bay Location's fleet consisted of a half-dozen Cessna 182s that took care of passenger and air cargo transport, while two larger Caravans saw to heavier loads. The office was located in one end of the hangar, which was empty now except for a sleek twin-engine craft that was in for repair. Julia had mentioned Abbot employed thirty people, mechanics, office staff and pilots, and the day started early. They both wanted to be in the air before the first employees arrived.

He found her outside the hangar, standing by the little white plane with red and black stripes running its length. Lights mounted under the wings illuminated both the ground and Julia, who was glancing at her watch. Both cockpit doors stood open. She motioned him around to the passenger door and climbed behind the wheel.

Within a few moments they were taxiing down the runway. Other than the lights marking their way and the tower lights, the world was black, the moon and stars hidden behind clouds. He concentrated on studying the instrument panel, dominated by two colorful LCD displays and half a dozen gauges. His boat navigation had sported nothing this sophisticated.

"This plane is a beauty," he said.

"George's new toy," Julia said. "He spent as much on avionics as on the aircraft itself. Inherited some money when his grandfather passed."

The plane lifted into the air. As Julia communicated with ground control, he put his head back against the soft leather seat and closed his eyes.

"Afraid of flying?" she asked.

He shook his head without opening his eyes. "No. Just tired."

"Go ahead and get some sleep. It'll take us most of six hours to get there. One of us might as well arrive rested."

He tried, but how could he sleep with so many thoughts running rampant through his brain? He tried to make sense of his aunt's behavior and that mysterious follow-up call. He couldn't. He tried to make sense of the attempts on Julia's life, but again, they were still shadowy maybes and ifs. He tried to reassure himself that Leo was safe, but that comfort eluded him as well.

Was it possible the police chief had something to do with this? Why would the man want Leo once Nicole was dead?

Nicole *was* dead, wasn't she?

He sat up straight. What if she wasn't dead? What if she'd staged her own death for some reason he couldn't fathom, and then she and her police chief boyfriend had kidnapped Leo?

Why? If she wanted to be thought dead and still have Leo, then why not stage both their deaths? Why this elaborate scheme?

Julia's voice cut through his thoughts. "What is it, Will? What's wrong?"

"Did you go to Nicole's funeral?"

"I was told she wasn't having one. I was told her body would be cremated and interred by her mother as per instructions."

"Then you never saw her body?"

"No. Why?"

"How do we know she's dead?"

Julia took a moment to answer. "Monsieur Pepin called me. He'd seen her body. He was the one who identified her. He said she suffered terrible injuries to her face and spine when the steering mechanism on her car broke. He said it appeared she died instantly. Leo was still strapped into his car seat in the back. The guy following her saw the accident and stopped. He was a doctor."

Will twisted his mind around that. Nicole mutilated, dead. His Nicole, the woman she had once been, a stunning bride, eyes full of hope and promise. Beautiful, vibrant, loving. At first.

Could Pepin be in on it, too? Hard to picture the correct little man getting tangled up in something this bizarre, and yet Leo had disappeared while under his protection. Plus they only had Pepin's word for it that the papers he said were given to him as proof of identification by the abductors were given to him and not brought by him. The police were fingerprinting them—would they find prints other than Julia's and Pepin's?

It didn't make any sense. None of it made any sense.

She touched his arm. "Try to sleep, Will. You're exhausted."

"How did you come to be a pilot?" he asked. He couldn't sleep, couldn't bear the image of his infant son caught in a giant spiderweb.

"One of my foster fathers was a pilot. He took me up a few times and I was hooked."

A foster child. Did that explain the sense

of loneliness she carried with her? "How long did you stay with this man and his family?" he asked around a yawn.

"Not long. I was a teenager by then and quite a handful. His wife didn't like me and I didn't like her. Her husband had to make a choice. I understand now that he made the right one."

"But at the time—"

She cast him a quick glance. "Not at the time. No."

"So you took flying lessons?"

"After high school I got a job at the Madrone airport. I met George Abbot and worked my way through flying lessons by working around his office. After I got my instrument rating, he hired me as a flight instructor. One of my students bought a King Air turbo so I got some experience with turbine as well as piston engines. I've been working for him for almost four years now."

There was a note of affection in her voice when she said Abbot's name that touched Will. He thought back to the way she'd sought comfort in Abbot's arms and now he understood.

"I was right, you are a woman who can change her own tire."

"Yes."

Closing his eyes again, he felt a sense of peace come over him that startled him at first. Peace? But the quiet hum of the engine and Julia's proximity were comforting. She was almost a different person now that she was up in the air, in control of the plane. The aura of isolation that seemed second nature to her on the ground seemed less profound up here.

There was also the fact that they were flying northeast in a more or less straight line. There was nothing he could do to make them go faster. At least he was going in the right direction to find Leo—he felt that in his gut.

Heaven help him if he was wrong.

JULIA COULD TELL it was close to eight in the morning from the busy freeway they flew over on approach. Rush hour was well under way. Will woke up as the plane rolled to a stop.

"Morning," she said.

He rubbed his eyes. "Morning." He looked out the window and frowned. "This is Spokane? I was expecting something bigger."

She gathered up the flight information. "I flew into Jack Cantor's place, a little airfield outside of Spokane. We were running low on fuel. Don't worry, I called Spokane, they know I changed airports. Jack's is less crowded plus Jack is a good friend of George's. I'll be right back. I just have to check in with him and find out where he wants me to park the plane."

It felt good to stand after hours of sitting. She'd had plenty of time to think while Will slept and the earth passed under her wings, a dark blur until the sun began to rise in the east, casting fiery fingers across the mountains. She'd also had time to study her passenger at close range without him knowing about it.

She liked his face. Not just because he was good-looking, not just because his features were strong without being overpowering. He had the look of integrity, possibly misleading to be sure; monsters didn't always look like monsters. She knew that. But every word out of his mouth, every expression in his eyes, every gesture reassured her that he was who and what he said he was.

And in his sleeping face she'd found further proof: in repose, she was reminded of Leo. Leo looked so much like his mother in coloring that it was hard to see his father in him until Will closed his gray eyes and shadows blurred his hair color. Even the light fuzz on his unshaven cheeks helped the illusion as it softened the angles of a man's cheekbones and jaw as compared to a baby's. The shape of Will's nose, the sweep of his lashes on his cheeks, even his ears, all resembled Leo.

Leo. The reason they were here. She picked up her pace.

"Hey, Jack," she said as she walked into the open hangar from which she'd heard the clinking and clanking of tools. Jack, greasy from his fingertips to his elbows, was working on an aircraft engine. He grabbed a grease rag from his pocket and wiped at his hands as he walked toward Julia. His John Wayne swagger reminded Julia of a cowboy, not a pilot.

"Julia." His gaze flashed over her head as he added, "Is George with you?"

"No, although I do have a passenger. I need to leave George's plane with you for a few hours and maybe rent a truck or something. Can you help?"

"You can take the blue Ford over to the

side of the building out there," he said, still wiping off the grease. "Sit down a spell and tell me how George is doing. You two still dating?"

"No, not anymore."

"Oh, I'm sorry to hear that."

"Neither one of us are, Jack. George has a new lady friend he's crazy about. Listen, I'm sorry to rush you, but I'm in kind of a hurry."

His expression turned brisk. "Then leave the Skyhawk right where you parked her. I'll get one of the boys to tie her down for you. Keys are in the Ford."

"Thanks a lot," she said. "She'll need to be refueled, too." Julia put out her hand to shake his but he laughed.

"You don't want to shake this greasy paw, sweetheart. I'll take a rain check."

Will was out of the plane, waiting for her. She pulled off the blue jumpsuit, revealing the red turtleneck and blue jeans she'd put on before she left the house. Stowing the jumpsuit in the plane, she grabbed her leather jacket and big shoulder bag.

It was a beautiful, bright day, but it was cold. When they got to the truck, Will walked around to the driver's door.

"Are you forgetting you don't have a license?" she asked, pausing by the back of the truck.

"I've had sleep, you've had none."

Further argument died on Julia's lips. Who cared who drove as long as they got going?

The truck was older than Julia by a year or two, dented and patched, cluttered with old fast-food wrappers and abandoned clothing. It was the airfield truck and Julia knew the engine was as perfect as the body was rusty. She climbed into the passenger seat, shaky with fatigue.

"Hungry?" she asked as he started the engine and backed away from the building.

"Not really."

"I need coffee. Let's stop somewhere and get something we can eat while we drive. My treat."

They found a fast-food restaurant, the same one represented by the majority of the garbage in the cab, and ordered large coffees and breakfast burritos. While she peeled back wrappers and sugared her coffee, he spread a map he found in the door pocket over the steering wheel. Julia heard him mumble to himself as he attempted to find the roads that would take them to his aunt's house.

The drive was an easy one as they took back roads not traveled by commuters, following a narrow, meandering river until they passed a green bridge leading over a bend in the river.

"That's it," he said, stopping the truck on the deserted road and backing up.

"How long has it been since you visited your aunt?"

"Not that long, but it was dark and she was driving."

"Then this isn't the house in which you grew up?"

"I grew up in a dozen houses, from Maine to Florida to Oregon. Aunt Fiona moved here after I graduated from college."

Julia thought for a moment. Will's aunt became a bigger enigma every time her name was mentioned. "I don't understand, Will. What was she running from? Why did she stop all of a sudden?"

He shook his head as he turned the truck toward the bridge. "She would never tell me. Truth is, the older I got, the less patient I became with her. What big dark secret was she hiding from me? Did it have to do with my past? If it didn't, then why all the secrets about my father and the rest of my family? And why did it stop when I left home and became an adult?"

"You have no idea?"

"I have one idea. It doesn't make a lot of sense, but it's the only thing I can think of."

"And that is?"

He spared her a glance as they rattled over the old bridge. "I think maybe my father had mob connections that threatened my safety."

"What suggested such a thing?" she asked.

Frowning, he drove down a small lane, flowering cherry trees dancing in the breeze, pale petals falling like snow. "Nothing. I told you it's goofy. I just can't think of anything else."

"But the mob—"

"I know, I know. It's a cliché, isn't it?"

"Well, yes, kind of. Plus your last name is Chastain. Doesn't sound very mob-like."

"But Chastain isn't my real last name," he said. "My aunt was a pro when it came to securing new identities. I can remember being William Noble, William Markham and who knows what else before I was old enough to care what my last name was."

Julia laughed.

"What's so funny?"

"It's just that your childhood sounds as screwed-up as mine."

He smiled back at her. "This mob idea is relatively new, kind of postcollege. When I was a little kid, I dreamed of a father who would move heaven and earth to find me. A secret spy. Or a superhero."

"Your basic preadolescent male fantasies."

"Yeah. But he never came. So then I decided he wanted to but couldn't. He was injured or being held prisoner in some dank jungle prison."

"Did you consider the thought that he might be dead?"

Will nodded. "Sure. But then we kept moving. So if he was dead, who was after us?"

"Maybe someone was after your aunt," Julia said. "Maybe you were just a little kid caught up in her drama."

"Maybe," he said.

The lane emptied into a large grassy parking area free of cars. A house sat at the back of the area, split-level construction of wood and glass, decks sweeping toward the river beyond. A well-tended orchard lay to the south of the house while trees towered over the roof. Blue wildflowers grew along the low gray rock wall, while borders of pink and white tulips surrounded the deck. A wheelbarrow and shovel sat off to one side along with a half-dozen shrubs waiting to be planted.

Despite the bucolic surroundings, Julia's stomach bunched into a knot around the burrito. Was Leo here?

Please let him be safe in this house…

"My aunt's car must be in her garage," Will said. "I can't believe she didn't come outside to greet us. She's turned into quite the gardener, puttering out here for hours at a time."

"Maybe she's asleep—"

"No. There's a buzzer in the house that's activated when someone crosses the bridge."

Alarm bells screeched in Julia's head. "Then why did we drive over the bridge and announce our presence to whoever else might be here with her? Why didn't we find a way to cross on foot?"

"There's no way to approach this house on foot or in a vehicle without tripping some kind of alarm, Julia. Aunt Fiona is a suspicious soul. Her motto is expect the worse then be surprised when it doesn't happen."

They both got out of the truck. Birds sang from the trees, sun glittered off the windows. Will came around the truck to Julia's side and caught her shoulders in his hands. Looking down at her, he said, "Stay here, okay? Let me scout this out."

She turned her face up to his. For an instant, electricity arced between their lips, between their eyes, connecting them, drawing them together. In that instant, she was reminded of the many times he'd touched her since they'd met, and despite the unbearable anxiety about Leo's safety that permeated every breath she took, the feel of his hands on her shoulders radiated comfort and strength.

She'd never felt like this before. Never felt part of something bigger than she was. Never trusted another person to hold up his or her share, to allow her the freedom and privilege of holding up her own. A fleeting fear of betrayal scampered through her mind, reminding her that she didn't know Will, that until meeting him, she'd heard few good things about him.

Their proximity seemed to alarm him in

the same instant it did her. He dropped his hands and she stepped away. "I have to come with you," she whispered. "Don't ask me not to."

"I wish I had a gun," he muttered, but that was all he said. She walked beside him as they crossed the grass and climbed the broad steps leading up to the front deck.

The door was solid, but glass panels on either side allowed them to peer all the way through to the back. Julia could see an expanse of dark wood floor and the edge of a rug. Everything looked tidy—and empty.

Will pulled the heavy door open. "This isn't good," he said. "My aunt isn't the kind of woman to leave a door unlocked." He called her name as he shut the door behind them.

There was no answering voice. They scanned the living room and kitchen, both of which were well-kept, before climbing a short flight of stairs to the rooms on the second level.

They found her lying faceup in a tangled bed, dressed in blue pajamas, a thick white comforter on the floor. Will called out, "Aunt Fiona?" from the doorway and when she didn't react, strode to her side.

Salt-and-pepper hair framed a white face. Will lifted her hand as he knelt beside the bed, then he felt her throat with his fingers. A moment later, he closed his eyes.

What had happened? Julia's gaze went to the bedside table where a prescription bottle sat beside a half-full glass of water. As Will set his aunt's hand back atop her still body, Julia walked into the bathroom, drawn by the clutter on the drain board she could see through the open doorway.

An empty glass vial and a syringe lay next to a glucose meter and test strips.

One of the foster families Julia had lived with had had a diabetic child. Julia recognized the paraphernalia. Had Will's aunt suffered an insulin overdose, sending her into a diabetic coma?

She turned back to the room in time to see Will lifting the prescription bottle using a tissue wrapped around his fingers. A jolt of uneasiness arched through her body. Why was Will being careful not to leave finger-prints?

"Sleeping pills, prescribed to her," he said.

"What's going on?" Julia said, struggling to control the fear that roiled in her stomach. That burrito had been a bad idea. She straightened her shoulders and added, "I'll call an ambulance—"

"No," he said, his face etched with resolution.

"But she needs—"

"She's dead. No ambulance or doctor can save her now, Julia. And we can't afford to allow ourselves to become tied to this house. If her death wasn't the accident it's supposed to look like—"

"But she's a diabetic. Will, she must have given herself a shot then taken a sleeping pill. If she went into shock while she was asleep, she could have died without ever regaining consciousness—"

"My aunt is the most careful diabetic in the world," he said, his voice as hard as granite. "She tests herself before every shot. And you're forgetting the fact that she wasn't alone here last night. Someone she didn't want me to know about, someone she didn't want to know about me, was here with her."

Julia took a step toward him. "Are you sure you're not being paranoid?"

"Aunt Fiona's conversation with me last night was stilted," he insisted, staring down at his aunt's lifeless form. "I thought she was just annoyed with me at first, for not telling her I hadn't died in the boating accident. I couldn't blame her for that. But she never asked a single particular. She never called me by name or alluded to our relationship. She answered with yes and no, then she threw out our rusty old code. It's too much. I don't believe this was an accident. All someone had to do was make her take a sleeping pill and then shoot her with more insulin than she needed. No doubt there's no way to prove she was murdered, but I don't believe her death was an accident."

And Julia realized she didn't either. Too much had happened over the course of the last twenty-four hours. This tragedy was just another in the string of catastrophic events that had begun with Leo's abduction.

Or had it started earlier, with Will's boating accident?

The fear now clawed its way up her throat. Who could be doing this? Why?

Will lifted his aunt's head and slid a chain from around her neck. Julia caught a flash of gold. A locket set with mother-of-pearl, she saw as he palmed it. He resettled Fiona's head back atop her pillow and stared at her a moment longer.

"She was a good woman who always tried her best to protect me," Will said as he gazed down at his aunt's face. "She didn't deserve this. Someone is going to pay."

"But first, Leo—"

"Yes," he said, a knot forming in his jaw. New resolve flooded his eyes. "First Leo. We need to check this house. Look for any sign a baby was here. Check the trash for diapers or mashed-up food, that kind of thing. Don't touch anything without a cloth or tissue around your fingers. Just in case."

They split up and went through each room. Julia found a framed picture on top of the television of Will holding Leo at about six months. The baby wore the booties Julia had made for him in her one and only excursion into knitting. She smiled at the memory of his plump little toes.

Whatever doubt she'd had about Will's identity—and by this time, it was infinitesimal—fled. Julia's heart twisted in her chest as she stared at Leo's face.

Why the strong feeling that this small child's future was linked to hers? That his fate was in her hands, despite Will's involvement? A shudder shook her frame. She had a premonition she would be the one to save

Leo. And if that were true, what did it mean? Will would be the one—

But he wouldn't. Something would happen that would prevent it…

She rubbed her temple. Since when had she become psychic? Good grief.

Will caught up with her in the laundry room. "Anything?"

"No. You?"

"Nothing. I don't think he was ever here, but I'm positive the house was searched before us. Aunt Fiona was a neat freak and the drawers all seem disheveled. Who knows what they were looking for? The only thing I can think of is her mysterious box."

"What kind of box?"

He moved his hands, outlining a rectangular shape about a foot by two feet. "About this big. The keeper of her big, dark secrets. She always kept the box near her, locked and hidden, until this last move. This time she set up an elaborate code and made me memorize it."

He withdrew his aunt's gold locket from his pocket and pressed a lever, folding one side out and another down. "This, believe it or not, is the key that unlocks the box. You have to know it's a key, then you have to know about the box it unlocks, and of course you have to know where to find the box. I imagine it's still safe."

"And what's in the box?"

Irony toyed with his lips. "I don't have the slightest idea. The key to my past, I hope. Maybe the next clue as to where to find Leo. Maybe nothing. I just don't know."

"I don't understand, Will."

"I don't blame you. I helped her move into this house. That's the last time I saw the infamous box. She made me memorize the code and told me if anything ever happened to her I was to retrieve it. I haven't thought about it in years."

"But you think it might help us find Leo?"

"It's a place to start."

"Okay. How do we find this box?"

"We look for her address book. Black, about as big as your hand—"

"It's in her desk drawer," Julia said. "I saw it when I searched the living room."

They retraced their steps to the living room where Julia took the small address book from the top drawer of Fiona's desk, using a cloth she'd found in the laundry room to keep from leaving prints. Will sat down on the edge of the sofa. As Julia sat beside him, he said, "Help me check every address for a phone number that ends in the numbers 0121. That's the beginning of the chain."

He opened the book on his lap. Julia scanned the right-hand pages as Will scanned the left. Julia spotted the correct four digits several pages into their search.

"Pete Flanders," she read.

"Okay, now we flip to the last name of Pete."

Under the *P* they found Harry Ray Pete.

"Now Ray," he said, flipping the pages to *R*.

The next name was Cyrus Ray. Will asked for a paper and pencil which Julia retrieved from the desk. "Cyrus Ray, 101 Bell Avenue, Tandy, Washington," he read.

"What does it mean?" Julia asked as Will took the paper and pen from her.

"The man we want is Cyrus plus the name of the town, that means Tandy in this case. Cyrus Tandy. The address is the three middle numbers of the phone number right above this listing, in this case, Sherry Racine at 603-555-0000. The street address is the name of the original entry. In other words, 555 Flanders Street."

"Yikes."

He glanced up at her. "I tried to warn you she was a tad mistrustful."

Julia thought of this clever cautious woman taking a sleeping pill forced on her by an intruder. Would she do that? Had she had a choice?

"I just didn't realize," she said, shaky again with the images that bombarded her mind. "How do you know what city to look in?"

"She told me it would be local."

"Didn't she worry that the person she chose would think the box was full of diamonds and steal it?"

"She said she planned on showing her trustee what was inside so they didn't get any ideas."

"So we're not going to find jewels and cash."

"No. We're going to find something worthless to anyone but her and me."

He wrote down the information and replaced the address book, wiping the cover with Julia's cloth. "Whoever this guy is, he lives close by." He took the phone book from the drawer and looked for Cyrus Tandy. "I guess he doesn't have a phone." He flipped to the local maps in the front of the book. In a few minutes, he found Flanders Street. "It looks like it's a couple of miles from here."

Julia was halfway to the door. It was hard to believe this convoluted code would lead them to Leo, but her cell phone was quiet, meaning George Abbot hadn't intercepted a ransom call. Where else could they go?

"I have to get something first," Will said. As she followed him down the hall, he stopped and turned to face her. "Know what just occurred to me? Everyone I'm related to is now dead or missing. Aunt Fiona. Nicole. Leo. Even you have been threatened three times."

"Nicole's death was an accident—"

"Was it? What if she didn't wrap her car around the tree by herself? What if she had help? What if Leo was supposed to die at the same time, but he lived, so had to be taken."

"That would mean they want Leo…dead," she whispered, her eyes welling with tears.

"Yes," Will said. "That would mean they want Leo dead."

Chapter Five

Before he left the house, Will moved a chair to the open bedroom closet in the spare room. He climbed on top and handed down three hat boxes and a half-dozen boxes of shoes to Julia who stacked them nearby. He then slid open the hidden panel behind the shelf and took out an old-fashioned cigar box.

"If you never lived here," Julia asked as he handed her the cigar box, "how did you know about this?"

"Hand me the hat boxes," he said, watching her as she put the cigar box on the bed and started handing him back everything he'd taken off the shelf. He said, "When I helped her move, she asked me to modify this closet. I knew what she intended to put up here. She made certain I knew." He wiped each surface Julia or he had touched before climbing off the chair.

"Your aunt liked boxes."

"Yes, she did." After replacing the chair and closing the closet door, checking to make sure everything looked as it had when they entered the room, he picked up the cigar box.

"So what's in this one?"

He opened the lid and smiled when Julia's breath caught. "Aunt Fiona's emergency money. She's kept twenty thousand dollars in this box for as long as I can remember."

If the present situation didn't qualify as an emergency, he didn't know what did. Besides, all this was his now. The house, the land, the money…everything. And all worth zilch unless he had Leo.

The thought struck him like thunder.

He turned to Julia, mind racing, words spilling out as he spoke. "What if someone knew I wasn't dead? What if they killed Aunt Fiona to make it look as though she died by accident? All her belongings come to me and that includes a staggering bank balance, that trust I mentioned earlier. What if her death is to assure that I have the means to ransom Leo?"

She stared at him, her eyes wide and dark and fathomless. "But it will take months to clear probate, for you to inherit."

"Maybe whoever has Leo is patient."

Julia bit her lip. "Okay, let's try to make sense of this. Someone tries to kill you. Nicole dies. Leo is sent to me. Someone tries to kill me while someone else picks up Leo at the airport. There had to be at least three people involved. The man who shot my tire plus the man and the woman who kidnapped Leo."

"We only have the lawyer's word about who picked up Leo."

"No, I didn't tell you, but the people who work at the airline told the police they saw Pepin talking with the people he described. And wait, Will. The reason you thought your aunt was involved was because of the so-phistication of the forged papers. She seemed to be the only one with the connec-tions and the guile to do such a thing. You thought the ensuing violence might be con-nected to one of the people who worked for her, someone who went off on a tangent. What if part of the tangent happened when they got here with Leo and your aunt threw a fuss about the aggression and they then found out you were alive? She was a wealthy woman and a threat, so they came up with plan B, which was to keep Leo, kill your aunt and ransom Leo back to you."

Will considered what she'd said. It made as much sense as anything else. "I think we'd better get out of this house."

Will said a silent goodbye as they drove away. It galled him to leave his aunt's body for others to find, but he couldn't afford the time it would take to wait for an ambulance and perhaps the police. If there were any questions about how she died, that would eat up still more time. He wasn't known in this town and he had no identification. He had to leave her as he'd found her, knowing she would urge him to find Leo, knowing she would say her body was just a shell, her spirit was no longer on the earth.

And there was another ugly fact to consider. As her sole heir, who had more cause to kill her then he did? Had someone noticed a blue truck ambling down the road this morning? Perhaps someone else saw his or Julia's face. If an autopsy was performed and if the coroner's verdict was murder, they would be prime suspects. He wasn't even sure he'd wiped every surface they'd touched before finding her body. His prints might be explained away by past visits, but Julia's?

He had to get her away from the house and take their chances.

They took the truck back across the bridge, Julia behind the wheel. Will took a few smaller bills out of the cigar box and stuffed them in his pocket. He said a silent thank-you to his aunt for her forethought. The woman had always been prepared to walk away from home at a moment's notice. But she hadn't walked this time. The one time it mattered the most, she'd allowed the enemy to get close.

The enemy. Who?

The box went under the seat.

"Flanders Street should be right along here somewhere," he said, glancing up as they passed a sign with a name he recognized from the map. It was still rural, still trees and fences with a glimpse of river now and again. They found Flanders Street within a mile and turned east. The street soon turned into a one-lane gravel road. Potholes filled with water announced it had rained sometime during the past twenty-four hours. Though Julia drove with what he was beginning to recognize as her trademark speed and agility, Will couldn't shake the feeling they were on a wild-goose chase, that Leo was moving farther and farther away to a place Will would never be able to find.

She braked the truck to an abrupt stop. A log cabin stood in front of them. "I'm calling George on his cell phone," she said. He waited for her to connect the call. It was obvious by the few words she spoke that nothing had happened.

But, then, he hadn't expected it would. Except that if his aunt didn't have Leo, who did?

"The police are suspicious of me leaving without contacting them," she said as she flipped off her phone.

There was nothing to be said to that. Of course they were. If they tried to trace her and found she hadn't followed her original flight plan, they'd be even more suspicious. By the time this was over, he and Julia would no doubt be found guilty of some heinous crime and would spend the rest of their lives in prison. If he failed to find Leo, he didn't care where or how he spent his life. But it wasn't fair for Julia.

He caught her arm as they approached the log cabin and she turned to look at him. He started to tell her she should fly home, she should leave finding Leo to him, it wasn't her problem, etc. But he couldn't. This meant as much to her as it did to him. He wasn't sure why, just that it did.

With an impulse driven from deep inside, he leaned down and touched his mouth to hers. Her lips were sweet, tender, soft, her response split-second. The kiss was over in an instant, but it upped the ante for both of them. He could see that when he backed away a little and looked in her eyes.

"Someday," he said.

She nodded as she flashed an uneasy smile.

An old man with a gray beard and matching collar-length hair stepped out of the cabin while they were still twenty feet away. He wasn't carrying a rifle though he sure looked as though he owned one. "Howdy," he said, coming down a set of rickety stairs.

His clothes—threadbare jeans and a green flannel shirt, cowboy boots and a corduroy jacket—looked as wrinkled and old as the man. He stuffed his hands in his pockets as he crunched his way across the gravel yard.

"I'm looking for Cyrus Tandy," Will said.

"That's me. What can I do you for?"

"I'm Fiona Chastain's nephew," Will said.

The old man's eyebrows shot up his forehead. "She said you might come someday."

"The day has come," Will said. "I need her box."

The old man licked thin lips. "She told me to keep it safe."

"And did you?"

"Damn straight I did. Can I ask where she got to?"

"She died," Will said. "An accident."

"Ain't heard no sirens or nothing."

"That's because I didn't call anyone, Cyrus. I was kind of hoping you might do that after you give me her box."

Cyrus's grizzled eyebrows made another trip up his forehead.

He nodded once, sizing up Will, his gaze darting over Julia. "Stay here." With a grunt, he turned and retraced his steps to the porch where he snatched a shovel from where it leaned against a rail. "Gonna have to take a little bit of a drive in your truck," he said as he returned.

"Is it far? We're in a hurry—"

"Get there faster if we start out now," he said. "Don't worry, it ain't far."

They all walked back toward the truck. The old man climbed up in the truck bed and settled with his back against the cab, shovel across bent knees. Julia slid behind the wheel and Will got in the passenger seat, sliding the back window open in order to hear directions, impatience all but over-whelming him.

Julia turned the truck around. Once back to the main road, there was an infuriating series of turns and switchbacks on little roads that seemed to go nowhere. Will began to wonder if the old man was addled.

The suspicion was heightened when Cyrus Tandy told them to pull off the road. Julia did what he said. There wasn't a building, a human, a cow—anything—in sight. Just trees and one of those little roadside crosses complete with a plethora of faded plastic flowers and a black-and-white photo of a middle-aged woman sporting an old-fashioned hairdo. The photo was pro-tected from the elements by a sealable plastic bag and thumbtacked to the cross.

Will got out of the truck and slammed the door a little harder than necessary. The old man climbed down from the bed, using the shovel to balance himself. Julia stood nearby, looking calm and collected.

"This here's where my Martha met her maker, God rest her soul," Cyrus said. "Twenty years ago now. The Rodney kid, drunker than a skunk, took her out whilst she was returning from a quilting bee up at Rosie Parker's place. Damn shame. She was a fine cook."

Will stared at the cross. Were they there to pay respects? How did he move the old man along without risking his cooperation?

"'Bout time to replace her picture. Had me a hundred printed up. The sun and rain are hard on the plastic bags."

Julia said, her voice soft and almost reverent, "You must have loved her very much."

"Married for thirty years. Got used to her. Still miss her." Thrusting the shovel into Will's hands, he added, "Dig."

Will looked at the stony ground around the small monument. At the cross. At the woman's picture.

"It ain't her grave, boy. She's buried up to the cemetery. This here is just a marker. When Mrs. Chastain give me that box of hers, I decided to bury it where my Martha could keep an eye on it for me. Now dig. Shouldn't be hard since your aunt give me a hundred dollars to dig it up for her a few weeks ago. Buried it again a couple days later. Got bursitis in my shoulder, though. Don't fancy a repeat performance. Dig right under them flowers. Best to move the pile of rocks first."

Julia knelt to clear away the flowers, holding them like a garish wedding bouquet when she stood. Will kneeled down and moved the rocks, then standing again, sank the shovel into the earth. It was easy going but it still took five minutes of effort to hit metal. He scooped out the last of the dirt and rocks with his hands and uncovered a box wrapped in heavy plastic.

He'd last seen the box years earlier when he'd helped his aunt move into her current house. This was the first time he'd hefted it, however. Always before it had been a hands-off proposition for him. It was lighter than he'd expected.

Will took off the protective plastic and deposited it in the back of the truck. Years of moves had worn the black paint off the box in spots, though the intricate handmade lock that went with the matching locket/key looked good as new.

"Them papers inside important?" Cyrus asked.

Will shrugged. "I don't have the slightest idea. Thanks for taking care of it for her." As Julia filled in the hole and replaced the flowers, Will dug a hundred-dollar bill out from the wad he'd liberated from the cigar box and handed it to the old man. "I know she'd want you to have this."

"Thanks. Been thinking 'bout what you said, 'bout you wanting me to call in her death. Look funny if I showed up at her place seeing as we didn't visit each other often. But Rosie Parker cleans for your aunt. I'll give her a call and tell her to go on over."

Julia said, "Rosie Parker. The lady your wife was visiting the day she died?"

"That's right. Old as the rest of us now, but still likes to clean for folks. Rosie told your aunt 'bout me. Said I was a man of character. Imagine that. Anyway, old Rosie likes a little extra cash to buy fabric. Crazy 'bout quilts. I'll call her."

"She shouldn't go to my aunt's house alone," Will said.

"She can get that worthless son of hers to

drive her over. Say she came for her pay or something. Don't worry, we'll get your aunt taken care of proper like."

Will fought the urge to explain the situation, but without knowing who was who in the grand scheme of things, decided it was better not to say too much. He smiled to himself as he realized how his aunt would have applauded his newfound caginess. It just made him feel sleazy.

"Your aunt said if you ever came for that box that was good enough," Cyrus Tandy said as he scratched at his unshaven cheek. "No proof needed, no nothing, just make sure you got it. Told me to trust you. Said you wouldn't come unless you had to."

"She was right," Will said. "Appreciate it if you leave us out of this for the time being."

Cyrus nodded. "Figured that."

Will put the box on the floor of the cab and climbed in after it. They dropped Cyrus off at his cabin with his promise to get things moving.

Despair enveloped Will as they drove back down the dusty road. His aunt gone, his last few years with her wasted as though he had all the time in the world to figure her out. He was honest enough to admit he'd been frustrated with her for most of his life, resenting the endless moves without explanation, her unyielding refusal to discuss his past, even when he was no longer a child.

Beside him, Julia sighed. Was she as worried as him that this would all turn out to be a colossal waste of time, that he was indulging his obsessive aunt and his own morbid curiosity when he should be…well, should be doing what? Storming the FBI?

That would go over well. He could waltz in and declare himself not dead, his son abducted by persons unknown, for reasons unknown, his aunt murdered, his world falling apart. ID? No, sir, but go head, take my fingerprints and see if they match one of a half-dozen aliases I've used through the years.

No, he needed to know if his past was culpable, or if it could be. Because without a clue as to where to search next, he was left with a host of wild suppositions.

What *did* make sense? His aunt orchestrating this elaborate scheme and dying when the tables turned on her? Nicole running around shooting at people, killing people?

Crazy.

And yet Nicole had set him up to be murdered. There was no one else who could have predicted his actions so spot-on. She wanted him out of the way. She wanted every dime he had. And she wanted their son all to herself. If she could do that, couldn't she do the rest?

If this didn't pan out, if the box was full of worthless mementos, then he'd have to go about uncovering the truth without indulging his fury.

The truck hit the main road, the ride became smoother. Julia sped up.

"I think you'd better find somewhere off the beaten track and stop the truck," he said. "It's time to find out what's in the box."

THEY MADE IT halfway back to the airport before Julia found a shaded wayside right off the road. Beer cans, cigarette stubs and food wrappers littered the ground, marking it as a teenage hangout after dark. It was late afternoon, the day eaten up with one event after the next. And the box that sat on the floor under Will's legs was as much a presence in the truck as if it had been a four-hundred-pound sumo wrestler.

With an air of anticipation, Julia watched

Will convert the locket into a key and insert it into the intricate lock.

He opened the lid and stared at the contents for a moment before an abrupt laugh escaped his mouth. He looked up at Julia and said, "Look at this."

Julia found a paper lying across the top of what looked like stacks of envelopes. In bold lettering, the paper said, "Ha! I knew you weren't dead!"

"It's dated two weeks ago," Will said. "She must have added this paper when she had Cyrus Tandy dig up the box." He folded the paper and stuck it in his jacket pocket, a fond smile still toying with his lips. Then he set the box on the seat between them.

Julia stared at the layers of stuffed envelopes. It looked like a poor man's filing cabinet.

"We'll take it one at a time," Will said.

She caught his hand. "Will, curious as I am, this isn't any of my business. I mean, your aunt went to such extraordinary measures to hide this—I feel like an interloper. I'll take a walk—"

He put his hand over hers. "Stay."

The first envelope held a birth certificate and passport for a person by the name of

William Olsen. The passport was stamped thirty years before. The second envelope held similar identification, this time in the name of William Markham. "I remember this name," Will said. "It followed me through grammar school. The next envelope should be Noble."

"How did she do this?" Julia asked as Will opened the largest envelope yet. "Everything looks so authentic."

"Connections," he said as a puzzled expression settled over his face. He was holding a stack of passport folders. He added, "If you have enough money, you can change your identity at will."

"Amazing," Julia said.

Will whistled as he opened folder after folder. "Look at this. She renewed my William Noble passport. Heaven knows where she got the right sized picture of me. There's even a whole stack of driver's licenses, one every few years, and here's the social security card. And a bank card. The PIN is good old 0121."

Julia picked up another folder, this one burgundy in color with gold embossing on the cover. "A college graduation certificate under the name William Noble. Did you attend Oregon State University?"

He took it from her. "Yes, but I graduated under the name Chastain. She had a duplicate made under the name Noble. Good grief, she's maintained an alternate identity for me all these years."

"Your parents are listed as Susan and Gus Noble."

"Good old Sue and Gus. Haven't thought about those names in years. I went through high school claiming them as my long-lost parents, you know. I can't believe this."

"You didn't know about any of it?"

"I gave up the Will Noble identity when I was eighteen," he said. "By then, we weren't moving as often. She said one more time for good luck's sake, changed our name to Chastain and came west. I went to college. She moved to Spokane and bought the first house she'd ever owned. I kept the Chastain name until someone blew up my boat."

"What about your aunt's old identification papers?" Julia asked.

He opened another large envelope that had been stapled shut, shuffling through the papers for a few seconds. "Looks as though they're all here, too."

Julia lifted out an envelope that looked older than the others. It was sealed with red wax and bore no handwritten notes as to its identity. She handed it to Will who opened it with care. He extracted a birth certificate like the others. No passport this time.

Julia took the birth certificate when he offered it to her. "What was your aunt's real last name, Will? Do you know?"

"No."

"This one lists your mother as Michelle Wellspring. And it lists your father as Theodore Lévesque."

He took it from her. "Notice there's no other identification in with this. No passport or library card or anything. Maybe it's my real identity?"

"It kind of looks like it. That name Lévesque. Doesn't it sound familiar to you?"

He turned surprised eyes at her. "No. Should it?"

She shrugged.

"Aunt Fiona used to sing that old Beatles song to me, the one with Michelle in it," he mused. "I can remember hearing the melody over and over again when I was very small, like a lullaby. I've always loved the song."

Michelle, ma belle…

Had his aunt tried to keep his mother's name alive for him in this obscure way? It seemed to fit what Julia knew of Fiona's character: oblique, cautious. "What else is in the box?" she said at last.

"The next layer consists of letters," he said, lifting out a very small stack of letters held together with an aging rubber band. "Maybe love letters?"

Will couldn't keep the excitement out of his eyes as he took off the rubber band, then he paused for a moment. "Maybe they can help explain…things," he mused almost to himself, and yet he didn't open them.

Julia didn't blame him for his hesitation. She might not have had a family of her own since the age of three years, but she'd always known what had happened to them. That their decisions had left her alone in the world hurt—it would always hurt. There would always be a hole in her heart. But at least she'd known their names and their fates and in that sense, known who she was. And she'd had a grandmother who'd tried and a distant aunt and cousin who hadn't. At least she'd known….

The handwriting on two of the envelopes looked neat and precise. The third was type-written. Two were dated the year Will was born, he said, and were addressed to

Michelle Wellspring in Chicago. The last one had arrived a month after his birth and was addressed to Fiona Wellspring, also of Chicago. All of them were covered with foreign-looking stamps and originated from somewhere called Port Jewel, Montivitz.

Will tapped the return address. "Have you ever heard of Port Jewel, Montivitz?"

"Montivitz. Isn't that a little island in the Mediterranean somewhere? It's been in the news, something about dissension concerning an American airfield. The king is getting old and things are going to hell. But there's something else…"

He touched her cheek. "I've never even heard of the place and look at all the information you have."

"You don't spend your life hanging around airports. I read a lot of magazines and newspapers while I wait for cargo to be loaded or passengers to show up. Besides, I think the political problems in Montivitz are more or less new and you've been in hiding, not browsing the newspaper."

"Yes," he said, his fingertips brushing her lips.

Despite the urgency, despite the kidnapping and the death threats and Fiona's probable murder and the layers of puzzles in the box, for one blinding moment there was just him. Just his breathing, his warmth, his fingers lingering on her face, tracing her lips, his gray eyes delving deep into hers…

She caught his hand and, turning it palm upwards, kissed his fingers and laid her cheek against his palm.

He cupped her chin and, leaning forward, touched his lips to hers. For one indulgent moment she allowed her mind to run clear as spring water, euphoria overcoming everything else. Her hand went around his neck, his slid down her body, over her breasts, under her coat, around her waist, his fingers digging into her back, hot through the cotton fabric of her shirt.

A brilliant shaft of sunlight seemed to pierce a dark, shadowed place in Julia's heart, a bleak place. The intensity of it almost hurt. The fear of facing the dark again hurt more.

She buried her face against his neck, closing her eyes, fighting a sense of panic that obliterated the moment. She could feel his heart pounding as hard as her own.

His voice was soft against her ear. "Are you okay?"

She drew away to look up into his eyes. She'd known Will Chastain—or whatever his real name was—a little over twenty-four hours. It just seemed as if months had passed. She didn't know how to answer him.

"Maybe in the future…" he said, his voice trailing off, leaving that last whispered word to scream in Julia's ears.

She pulled farther away, fighting for something to wrap her mind around that wasn't as scary, as terrifying, as the future and Will's place in that future.

And that brought up thoughts of Leo and with those came the sobering fear that Leo might not be here in the future, they might never know what happened to him.

"What do we do if there's nothing helpful in those letters?" she asked.

He released her, his embrace lingering just a moment as he replied, "I thought about that. If nothing comes from the letters then I go back to Seattle and start getting my life back in order. I'll question the police chief. I'll tackle Monsieur Pepin. I won't give up until I find Leo and bring him home."

Julia nodded. How could she help but notice that she'd been left out of any of his plans?

And why shouldn't he leave her out? She was Leo's dead mother's cousin, he was Leo's father. She had no rights.

The thought created a deep ache. She settled back in her seat. She mustn't give in to self-pity. Her future was not only unwritten, it was uncertain and right now, unimportant. What mattered was bringing Leo home. Leo mattered.

A little of the old armor shifted back into place. She was here because of Leo, because of a conviction that she would be needed before the end. Julia, the psychic pilot!

"Julia? What's wrong?"

"Read the letters," she said, avoiding his gaze. "It's going to be dark soon."

She could feel him staring at her and she flashed a smile. He appeared confused. Nothing she could do about that. She added, "We can't afford to become distracted. We need to focus on Leo."

The air in the truck blew cold. His voice very low, he said, "I have not lost focus on regaining my son, Julia. I'm sorry. I'll watch my step from now on when it comes to… you…but please, don't remind me to think of my child again. He's never off my mind."

It was on the tip of her tongue to apologize, but she stopped herself. Better to keep a neutral expression. Better all the way around if he was annoyed with her. Easier, safer.

He opened the oldest letter.

"It's short," he said.

"Please read it out loud."

Without glancing at her, he began.

My dear Michelle,
Meeting you was the highlight of my American visit. The time we spent together will always remain in my heart. I am sorry I had to return home on such short notice, but as you know, my father has taken ill. Things do not look good for him.
Theo

"Short for Theodore, the name on your birth certificate, Will. This letter is from your father." The words in the letter filled Julia's head. She heard regret and lost love. What did Will hear?

"It appears that way. Where's home? This island called Montivitz?"

"I guess."

Will folded the letter back into its envelope and opened the second. "Another short one."

You will have heard by now that my father is no better and is, in fact, expected to die.

"Your grandfather," Julia said.

It is impossible for me to continue our relationship, indeed, I must request that you never again contact me directly. If you decide to keep your baby contact this number: Z56-P8 90 86. Ask to speak to Minister Poletier. He will arrange payments to take care of you and your offspring. This letter does not constitute acknowledgment of your claim and is made solely in the spirit of past friendship.
Theodore

Will said, "The bastard."
"He abandoned your mother."
"Never even took responsibility for her pregnancy. Guess he had to stay on his island and take over the family business."

The bitterness in his voice was like a slap of reality to Julia. Her own pique dissipated in light of how difficult these revelations had to be for Will. She could all but hear his childhood fantasies shattering into little pieces. "Want me to read the last one?" she asked.

Handing her the letter, he studied the envelope. "Looks like this Minister Poletier is getting into the act."

Due to the advancing day, the light in the cab was failing. Julia dug a small flashlight out of her shoulder bag and used it to high-light the letter.

"It's addressed to Fiona Wellspring."

Please accept condolences on the loss of your sister. The funds she agreed to before her death have been deposited as per her request. The following news is most distressing, but despite everything and against explicit directions to the contrary, there are several facts of which you must be aware.

The first is that the king—

Julia put the letter down on her lap, biting her lip as she gazed out at the fading sky.

Images from magazines and newspapers mingled with that last word—*king*. She gasped.

Will said, "What is it, Julia?"

"I remember where I've heard the name *Lévesque*. It's been in the news, on the television, in the tabloids. They called him Fabulous Freddy."

"You've lost me," he said.

"He was a prince."

Will's forehead wrinkled as he said, "A prince. What do you mean?"

"I mean a real live member of the aristocracy. Seventeen or eighteen years old, daring, the heartthrob of young girls everywhere. In the tabloids because he was always doing something crazy like dating some unsuitable foreigner or nightclubbing—rich kid stuff. The last thing he got into was extreme sports. A few weeks ago he tried to snowboard down the face of a mountain without a helmet."

"You're talking in the past tense."

"Because he didn't make it. He lost control and fell to his death. His name was Prince Federico Lévesque. But the press dubbed him Fabulous Freddy. The magazines were full of his funeral. His father is old but very powerful."

They stared at each other for a long moment before Julia said, "I think King Theodore Lévesque is your father, Will. And that means you're—"

"Don't say it," he warned, holding up his hand. "Just don't say it."

Chapter Six

She didn't have to say the actual words. They resounded, unspoken, unbelievable.

His father a king.

Did that mean Prince Federico Lévesque had been his younger brother?

How did this fit? What did it have to do with Leo? He was wasting time, losing focus, just as Julia had warned him. He had half a mind to take the wheel and drive to the airport. He had to do something, go somewhere, punch someone—

Julia said, "Are you ready for me to finish the letter? Do you want me to stop?"

He relaxed his fists, took a deep breath. "No. Go ahead, read."

Julia turned her flashlight back on the letter. "Okay," she said, finding her place.

…there are several facts of which you must be aware. The first is that the king has refused to become involved with Michelle Wellspring's child or any difficulties arising because of the birth of this child. He is aware the child is now motherless.

Will closed his eyes. This was his father. Saying Will's mother's death wasn't his problem, her abandoned baby not his problem. This was his father.

Julia must have sensed his withdrawal. She'd stopped speaking. "Just read the rest of the damn thing," he said. "Please."

Second, news of a royal heir has leaked to certain political factions within Montivitz. Be aware there are differences of opinion concerning the role of the monarchy within our own government. Claims to the throne are not to be taken lightly; our history is not without bloodshed in these matters. As a foreigner, you would not be welcome on Montivitz soil. Hence, the child, William Wellspring, could be in grave danger now or in the future.

Our law is clear. The first in line to succession is the first son of a reigning king's legal union. Second in line is a daughter produced in the same manner. Third in line is the eldest illegitimate progeny who can provide verification of his or her direct link to our king to the satisfaction of our parliament. After that, various cousins, etc.

Without validating your late sister's claim that King Theodore Lévesque is the father of her son, conscience compels me to issue this warning: use precaution, Miss Wellspring, when it comes to keeping your nephew's true identity and whereabouts a secret. There are people here who will stop at nothing to eliminate the threat this child could make to the throne now or in the future. There are ample funds available in your sister's estate to serve you in this undertaking. I have provided you with a means of contacting me and I would suggest you give me a means of contacting you so that I can issue any appropriate warnings.

In the future, when the king marries and produces a legitimate heir, all dan-

ger to William Wellspring will disap-
pear. Until then, vigilance!
A. V. Poletier
Ministry of Security
Port Jewel, Montivitz

Stunned into speechlessness, Will
watched Julia fold the letter along the
crease lines and put it back in the
envelope. If his head had been reeling
before, it now seemed stuffed full of dis-
illusions blanketed in a thick layer of thun-
derstruck disbelief.

"I now kind of wish my dad had been a
mob boss," he muttered.

Julia's lips curved. He was relieved when
she turned off the flashlight and didn't bring
out the next layer of papers from the box.
The cab resumed its twilight aura.

"I don't know what to say," she said,
"except that last I heard your father was still
alive."

"Who gives a damn? How does any of
this help me find Leo?"

Her voice was soft when she spoke. "The
timetable is interesting. Years ago, your aunt
got this letter after your mother's death and
began a life of subterfuge, financed with

what you thought was a trust but I bet was guilt money paid by your father. All this stopped when you turned seventeen, which just happened to be the same year your father produced a legitimate heir. Then Prince Federico dies and within days, all hell breaks loose in your life. But why wouldn't your aunt have known about the prince's death and put two and two together? Why wouldn't she have warned you before the boat explosion?"

"Aunt Fiona didn't even own a television," he said. "No newspaper subscription, no computer. After years of running, she'd turned into a land owner. Hiking, gardening, harvesting. I bet she didn't even know Federico Lévesque had died." He raced to get his thoughts in order. "This could relate to Leo after all."

"I think it has to, Will. It's just too much of a coincidence if it doesn't."

"So maybe Nicole and her lover had nothing to do with the attempt on my life," he said. His head had gone from reeling to aching. "Why would someone in Montivitz kidnap Leo?"

"Because he's your son and your father is getting old," she said. "In other words, you and Leo are both royal heirs. And everyone thinks *you* are dead."

"And that leaves Leo."

JULIA DROVE not to the airport but to a restaurant. Neither she or Will had eaten since breakfast and Will looked as though he'd just survived an enforced death march. They both needed time to think of what to do next. There were still unread letters and documents in the box. Who knew what further disasters awaited discovery?

After ordering the chicken Caesar salad, Julia excused herself to go call George's cell phone, choosing a small dark alcove near the back of the restaurant for privacy.

"Hey, George. What's up?" she asked.

"Julia. Where are you? The police—"

"You got a ransom call? Oh, George, what did they say? Is Leo okay? What do they want?"

"No ransom call," George said. There was a long pause during which Julia coped with the conflicting emotions of relief that no one had called and disappointment for the same reason.

"I didn't want to tell you over the phone," he said at last.

"Tell me what?"

"I thought maybe you and that guy would be back by now and I could talk to you in person. Or the police could—"

"Are you at my house now?" Unbidden, the image of her little house blossomed in her mind. She could picture George standing by the sliding glass door, peering into the darkening backyard or walking down the short hall. Maybe he was in the kitchen, heating water for coffee, the smiling daisy kitchen clock tick-tocking above his head. She missed every square inch of that modest house with a pang that shocked her with its intensity.

A long pause followed by a hesitant, "Sort of."

"What's going on?"

"I fell asleep this afternoon, after your call," he said, his voice low and urgent. "I woke up when I heard breaking glass. I was in your bedroom. I got out a window. If I'd nodded off in front of the TV, I wouldn't have made it out in time."

Julia's breath seemed suspended as she struggled to understand what he was saying. She mumbled, "If you'd been in front of the TV?"

"Someone blew up your house," George said, his voice gentle.

Julia's ears began to ring. She stared at a phone number scribbled on the wall next to her face and couldn't read a single number.

"Julia?"

"They blew up my house?"

"It's gone," George said. "Well, almost gone."

Her throat closed. George added, "The cops are all over it. They now think the little boy's disappearance has more to do with you than with him. They're asking everyone a ton of questions, looking into your past, interviewing people. I had to tell them about the bullet in your wall and the fact you'd been attacked. I mean, they were acting like you had something to hide. Like drugs. Questioning your routes and deliveries. They got a search warrant for Abbot Air. Of course, they didn't find anything."

"I'm so sorry—"

"Not your fault. I had to set them straight. I don't know if they believed me—"

"Tell them to look at the tire in my trunk," she said.

Another long pause before George said,

"Honey, there's not much left of your car. It was a big bomb."

Julia's head throbbed with grief. "Are you sure you're okay, George?"

"I'm fine. But they know you took the Skyhawk. I think they have a warrant out on you for questioning. I bet they'll be waiting for you at the airport—"

"I didn't land in Spokane, I went to Jack Cantor's place. I told Spokane, so the police will find out—"

"But it might take them a little longer. You need to come home and get this straightened out. The plane will be fine with Jack. You catch a domestic flight—"

"I can't afford the time to tangle with the police right now," she said, pushing images of her smoldering house out of her mind. "We have to keep moving to have any hope of finding Leo."

"It would look better if you went to them—"

"I don't care how it looks," Julia said. "It's Leo who matters. Promise me you won't tell them about Jack Cantor. They'll figure it out soon enough. I'm sorry for involving you, George," she added, her voice now shaky.

"Don't worry about me. But you should

ask yourself if you can trust the man you're with. Seems to me—"

"Be careful, George," she said. "Good-bye."

She folded her phone and went back into the restaurant. Dinner had been served. Will sat with his head in his hands, staring down at his hot turkey sandwich. Her salad looked wilted.

"We have to talk," she said, sliding into the booth across from him. "Things are more screwed-up than ever."

"Is that possible?" he said.

"Can you eat that?"

"No. You?"

"No."

He met her gaze and his eyes widened. "What happened? You're as white as a sheet. Is it Leo? Did George hear—"

"No," she said, gripping his hand. "It's not Leo. But we have to go."

Will paid the bill. Julia took his arm as they exited the restaurant, rushing him across the parking lot. She was sure a million eyes watched as she unlocked the door and climbed inside.

He turned to her. "What's going on?"

"Someone blew up my house last night. More or less demolished it."

"Is George—"

"He got out in time. No one was hurt. My car was still in the garage, though, so whoever blew up the house probably thought they were getting me. Or you."

Will put a hand around the back of her neck, pulled her close and kissed her forehead. "Plaster and metal can be replaced," he said. "At least no one was hurt."

Tears burned behind her nose. She'd never admit it to anyone but that house had been like a family member to Julia. Not just the house, either. Her inexpensive furniture—furniture she was still making payments on. All the little mementoes she'd managed to hold on to all these years were now rubble. The pictures of her grandmother. Her daisy clock! The tears spilled over her cheeks and she wiped them away with a furious motion. How could an insurance policy ever replace all those sentimental things?

But there were bigger fish to fry. "It gets worse," she said. "The cops have now decided that Leo's abduction has something to do with me and my life. They searched George's place for contraband. They think I was running drugs! They found nothing, of course. Sooner or later, though, they'll look at all the Spokane airports including Jack Cantor's strip and—"

"Let's get out of here," he said.

She started the engine and merged into traffic. She was so jittery she was afraid she'd crash into something. "I can't believe the police think I was involved in Leo's kidnapping."

"I'm sure they don't, Julia. Look at it from their point of view. You disappeared and your house exploded. The baby is gone with no attempt at ransom. We'll explain it to them later. It'll be all right."

"They'll find Jack Cantor's place soon. Jack will tell them we have this truck. The truck might lead them to your aunt and Cyrus Tandy and who knows what they'll extrapolate out of that."

"Calm down," he said, reaching for her right hand and anchoring it in his. "Take a deep breath. That's why we're going to abandon the truck."

"If they catch up with us, it will take years to get it all straightened out and meanwhile, what will happen to Leo?"

What she didn't add was the terror that filled her soul at the thought of being at the mercy of the system again. Of being told when and where to go. Of losing her freedom, being torn from what was left of her life. It was selfish even to think this way, but how did she stop these thoughts from coming on their own?

She couldn't. But she didn't have to give them a voice, and she struggled to regain control of her emotions.

"We'll disappear," Will said.

"I don't know how to disappear," she mumbled. "I don't know how to evade people and—"

His laugh startled her and she glanced at him. "Well, babe," he said, his eyes glimmering in the highway lights. "You just happen to be with a man who's an expert on all of the above. I learned from a pro. Pull over."

THEY PARKED in the crowded parking lot of a multiplex. Will could feel Julia's tension. His own had peaked and faded, leaving cold hard resolve in its place.

He made a list in his mind as he retrieved the false identity of William Noble from his aunt's box.

1. Get out of Spokane.
2. Search the rest of the box.
3. Get Julia out of this before it's too late.
4. Find Leo.

Short list.

He put several large bills in his pocket, then dumped the rest of the cigar-box money into the metal box. The truck held nothing else of theirs except their morning food wrappers which blended right into the many others littering the floor.

"We leave the truck here. Lock the keys in the glove box. You can't risk calling your friend, but the cops will trace the truck back to him soon enough and when this is over, you can apologize for the inconvenience. We'll stick some money in the glove box to cover the towing expenses. I'll carry the metal box. Put the cigar box in that oversized bag you tote around and let's go."

Will had chosen this parking lot not only because of all the other cars but because of its location on a strip of open-at-night businesses. The one he wanted was a mile away. He appreciated Julia's long-legged gait and the coiled energy he knew propelled her at his side.

Dan's Best Used Cars was located on a corner and consisted of a couple of dozen old cars in varying degrees of disrepair. An old white trailer seemed to function as an office. Leaving Julia in a donut shop with the metal box on the bench beside her, Will hiked onto the lot by himself. He'd kicked a few tires and opened and closed a few doors before a young salesman burst from the trailer and jogged onto the lot.

"Can I help you?"

Will stopped by a car with a price on the windshield of $2,500. Four doors, gray paint, tinted windows, domestic, not the kind of car to attract a second look from anyone. "If this thing runs, I'll give you two grand. Cash."

The kid grinned. He had a round face and a Cheshire cat smile. If he disappeared right now, his twinkling white grin would remain.

"It runs," the kid said. "I took it home last night. The tires aren't bad and it's clean. At least it's what Dan calls clean."

They took the car on a quick spin, and using the name and identification of Will Noble, Will bought the car. It smelled like stale smoke, but there was little he could do about that. The salesman threw in a hanging pine tree deodorizer.

Will drove to the donut shop where Julia stood outside on a gloomy corner, out of sight, the box at her feet. She didn't recognize the car, of course. One of the reasons he'd chosen it was the tinted windows. For a second, he took an impartial look at Julia Sheridan.

Glossy dark hair, loose from her ponytail for once, falling around her face and shoulders, face anxious but perfect, twice as pretty as she'd been the night before. She was becoming familiar to him, and for a second, he thought of the moment after those wild kisses when his world had been crumbling and he'd sought a moment's refuge in her arms.

And then he'd felt her body stiffen, her mind switch on.

Had she suffered some kind of abuse in one of those foster homes? Had some jerk come on to her—or worse? Was she afraid?

He should squash his growing affection for her. Squash it like a bug. Because of him, she'd lost her home, was wanted by the police. She'd been threatened on every level of her existence and yet there she stood, resolute and fierce, believing he was Leo's best chance, determined to see it through. He knew she wouldn't stop until it was over and her strength made him feel unworthy.

He now had her safety to consider as well as Leo's. In some ways it would be so much easier to do this alone without her to worry about. Though it wrenched him to consider it, the time would soon come to set her free, to get her out of this craziness. He didn't for a moment think the police suspected her of kidnapping Leo. He suspected they just wanted to question her, perhaps even protect her from harm.

As for him being the heir to the throne of Montivitz? He hadn't known the country existed a few hours before and now it looked as though his exalted identity had gotten his wife and aunt murdered, a woman he was growing increasingly fond of threatened and his son kidnapped, fate unknown.

He didn't care about being a king, but he did care if some imperial edict was out to decimate his family and those he cared for. He had to find Leo, he had to find the people responsible for Nicole's and Fiona's deaths, he had to make sure Julia got her life back.

For now he rolled down his window. "Julia?"

She jerked her attention his way. She didn't smile, just walked to the car, opened the back door and deposited the box, then slid into the passenger seat. The sigh that escaped her lips did everything but rattle her bones.

They were on their way north out of Spokane a minute later.

JULIA SAT rock-still with a smile pasted on her face as they approached the small border crossing into Canada. She had her passport ready. She always carried it when she traveled because of her job. Okay, truth was she always carried it because she always carried about half of what she owned. She'd learned to be prepared for life's curveballs.

And then the thought struck her. The bag didn't carry half of what she owned, it carried everything she owned. This was it. Clothes, toothbrush, flashlight, a few papers, random makeup, a paperback novel—this was it.

And, oh yeah, a bombed-out shell of a house on a tiny plot of land.

The guards looked at her passport without comment which reassured her there wasn't some kind of border alert out for Julia Sheridan, apprentice desperado. Will entered Canada as William Noble and what she lacked in aplomb, he more than made up for, joking with the guards, as comfortable as if he'd changed his identity every day of the week.

Of course, that had been more or less true for a great part of his life. No wonder his first reaction upon being almost blown to smithereens had been to play dead and see what happened next. It was second nature for him, a way of life dictated by the extreme circumstances of his birth.

But not for her. Her head pounded with the effort of looking carefree. She didn't take a steady breath until they'd been passed through and were on their way.

They found a motel a few miles further on and Julia sat in the car, worn out after a day where she'd witnessed so many new things and had her emotions yanked around like a hapless pup on the business end of a leash. She leaned her head against the cool glass window and closed her eyes.

Will opened her door, catching her shoulder when she fell against his thigh. She'd fallen asleep waiting for him to check them in.

"Come on, *Mrs. Noble,* we still have a full night ahead of us." He took her hand and helped her from the car, then retrieved the metal box. He handed Julia the key fastened to a red plastic disk and she slipped it into the lock on room 5.

The room was small and shabby. Faded red drapes, worn red bedspread, carpet of a different shade of red. A vibrator connected to the headboard promised titillating delights for the proper change.

"It looks like a bordello that's seen better days," she said.

"Much better days," Will answered. He put the box in the middle of the single queen bed and stretched. "Believe it or not, I'm hungry. I saw a store that looked open a couple of blocks from here. Mind if I go back for something to eat?"

"I'm going to take a shower," Julia said.

"Lock the door after me," he cautioned.

She took a quick shower and slipped on the blue sweatpants and shirt she'd packed for sleepwear. She had clean underwear, but she didn't have any more clothes so the turtleneck and jeans would have to take her through the next day.

She was sitting on the bed, staring into

space, when Will got back. He carried a plastic bag bulging with goodies.

"Grapes from Peru, bread baked fresh yesterday. Some kind of pasta-and-artichoke-salad thing from the deli. Cheese, salami and bottled water. Plastic knives and forks. Best of all, I found a pocket world atlas."

His aunt's box sat there on the bed like a giant squatting toad, promising more trouble, more heartache, but also the possibility of helping them figure out what had happened to Leo. Julia trotted into the bathroom for a clean towel which she threw over the box, transforming it into an impromptu table.

Will found Montivitz while Julia speared an olive in the pasta salad. "It's this little speck of an island," he said, squinting to see it. The atlas was just about the size of a paperback novel so everything looked tiny. "Surrounded by all the big guys," he added. "Algeria to the south, Spain to the east, Italy west, France kind of north."

As Julia chewed her olive, Will closed the atlas and tackled a piece of cheese. "It looks so insignificant, doesn't it?"

"I guess it's like the real estate people say. Location, location, location."

"So tell me what you remember reading about the politics of the place."

The pasta salad was so delicious she was in danger of hogging the whole thing. She handed the container to Will and munched on grapes as she tried to recall what she'd read. "There's an American airstrip there, built during the Cold War when the monarchy was sympathetic to America. I guess the current king, your father, has also been a supporter. But now there's a faction that wants to kick out the Americans. I gather the whole country is in an uproar since the king is elderly and there's no known heir."

No known heir. The words robbed both of them of their appetites.

Julia cleaned up the leftovers and trash as Will took a quick shower. He came back into the room wearing just the jeans, barefoot and bare-chested, drying his short dark hair on a towel, looking trim and muscular, damp and very sexy.

The feel of his lips on hers, his tongue sliding next to hers, his fingers gripping her back, brushing her breasts, the soft timbre of his voice, the urgent look in his eyes—it all came marching back into her mind with the conviction of an invading army. And in that moment, she understood something very basic.

She wanted him. She had since he'd caught her arm at the airport and she'd sensed the strong inner core that sustained him, amazing now that she knew more about him, knew that he'd been shuffled about and kept in the dark, knew that she'd met him just days after a murder attempt, after the loss of his son. Nevertheless, it was there, an inborn part of him, and she'd reacted to it from the first moment he touched her.

She whipped the towel off the box, anxious to get her thoughts back on track. "Your arm looks better," she said. "Except for the bruises. They're quite colorful."

"Let's get to it," he said.

They sat with their backs against the headboard, the box between them. Will opened it and took out the layers they'd already examined. Beneath were more envelopes.

"The saga continues," he said.

The first envelope in the new layer was yellowed with age. Photographs and slips of paper floated out when Will upturned it.

Their attention was drawn to the photo that landed on the top. A young woman with dark-gold hair stood next to an older man who looked enough like Will to cause a double take.

Will picked it up, turning it over to read the faded ink on the back. "Theo and me, Monterey, California, March, 1973."

"Your parents," Julia said.

"I was born in November. She must have already been pregnant when this picture was taken."

The woman was very pretty and very, very young. She wore her hair shoulder-length, caught in a clip on the right side, one hand raised as though to brush stray honey-gold strands from her eyes. The man looked to be in his early thirties, much the same age as Will now. Same square shoulders, same gray eyes. The trees behind them looked windblown.

Will studied it, not saying anything. Julia tried to imagine what it was like for him seeing his mother's face for the first time. And his father's.

After a while, he picked up another photo. This one was of two young women posed in front of a fountain of some kind. The same blonde as in the first picture, her hand looped through the arm of a taller, darker woman. Both wore smiles and sundresses.

"Aunt Fiona," Will said, touching the second woman with a fingertip. "It's hard to believe she was ever this young."

"She and your mother were beautiful. And they look so happy."

He set the picture aside.

What followed were dozens more photographs, all loose as though no one had had the time or the heart to put them in an album. Each was labeled, and as they went through them, one by one, Will met his family. His grandparents, still very much alive and not that old in 1972. Aunts and uncles. Cousins…a whole normal life of people and houses and pets and vacations.

"Do you think Fiona severed all ties with them when she took you after your mother's death?"

"It looks that way. From what I can gather looking at the inscriptions on these photos, there are tons of Wellsprings scattered across New Mexico and Arizona, an area of the country where we never lived." He was quiet a moment before he added, "I don't think I ever appreciated what my aunt gave up to raise me. She left her family, never married, never had a child of her own. She spent her whole life protecting me."

"I wonder why she didn't reconnect with the Wellsprings once your father married and produced a legitimate heir?"

He picked up a small envelope addressed to him. It had been lost among the photos.

"This is Fiona's handwriting. Maybe she'll tell me."

Julia looked over Will's shoulder as he unfolded the paper. It was dated a decade before.

William, it began.

Okay, kid, here's a photo gallery of the maternal side of your family. When your mother got pregnant out of wedlock and refused to divulge your father's identity, they turned their backs on her. I was there when you were born, I held Michelle when she died. She loved you very much and I promised her I would see you safely grown up and that's what I've tried to do. I haven't had contact with your grandparents and the rest of that sorry lot for decades. Now it's up to you to decide what you want to do about them. There's a book in here somewhere with their last-known addresses.

William, if you're reading this, I'm either addled or dead or something worse. Take care of yourself. Watch your back.

Much Love,
Aunt Fiona.

"Wow," Julia said.

He smiled. "How like Fiona. No real explanation, just puzzle pieces for me to fit together along with total faith I'd figure it out. But what does any of this have to do with Leo?"

"Look," Julia said.

The last photo had been lying facedown. Unlike the others, which were snapshots, this one looked cut from a magazine.

It showed Will's father sitting on a throne in front of a lattice-like wall of gold. Attendants in bright blue tunics stood at attention. Theodore Lévesque, dressed in a black uniform decorated with coils of gold braid and colorful ribbons, a sword at his belt, a crown glittering with stones on his head, looked regal, majestic and handsome as all get out.

He also looked a lot like Will would look if he dressed the same way except for the tilt of the head, the air of superiority and privilege Will's father wore with as much confidence as he wore his crown. For the first time, it struck Julia she was sitting on the bed with a man who could be king.

The typewritten caption read: Coronation of King Theodore of Montivitz. 1973.

"Your mother or aunt must have cut that out of a magazine."

Will said, "My mother. My aunt wouldn't have bothered."

They both looked into the box, but except for the old address book and a final fuchsia silk pouch, it was empty. Will brought out the pouch and opened it over his hand.

A dazzling heap fell into his palm.

Julia lifted the heap and held it up toward the light. It unfurled into a bracelet of platinum, rubies and diamonds, delicate but heavy, feminine and yet no doubt worth a king's ransom.

"Wow," Will said.

Julia held it up to the light. "It's gorgeous," she said.

"My father must have given it to my mother before he left the country. I wonder…"

Julia lowered her gaze. She could tell he

found comfort in this thought and she had no inclination to ruin it for him. She handed it back. "He must have cared," she said.

He caught her arm and draped the bracelet across her skin. The red jewels glimmered with imprisoned fire at odds with the icy cold of the diamonds and platinum. He fastened it around her wrist.

"Just what the well-dressed woman wears with a T-shirt," she said, but the truth was the glittering bracelet transcended her cheap clothes, the tawdry room, the weak light.

"My father must have given it to my mother before he left," he said again. For a second, his voice took on a speculative tone as he added, "I wonder how they met. I wonder why he left her and why, after he became king, he didn't help her. Though he did make sure she had money and a contact within the government."

Julia didn't know how to respond. It seemed Will was trying to come to some kind of peace with this father he'd never known. She'd spent most of her life trying to come to peace with her family; he deserved a few moments without her nay-saying.

"I mean," he said, "why would my mother

cut out a picture of his coronation and keep the bracelet if it wasn't because she cared and thought that despite appearances to the contrary, he cared, too?"

Julia was finding this take on Will's history kind of hard to swallow. What good was a gesture when no positive action followed?

"How does this help us find Leo?" she asked as she unclasped the bracelet. As a token of love, it was breathtaking. The beauty faded when you thought about what had come next: betrayal, death, loss.

"Just a minute," Will said as he dug through the other material in the box. He found the stack of letters and started reading them again. Julia began replacing things, starting with the bracelet in its pouch, then the photos and the envelopes.

"I know what to do next," Will said.

"What?"

"This number…"

"What number?"

He tapped one of the letters with a forefinger. "My father gave my mother a phone number for Minister Poletier. It was Poletier's job to help my mother. Later, he contacted my aunt with warnings, over and over again through the years, every time he caught wind of some crazy plot to murder me, right?"

"I assume so."

"So maybe my father assigned him to make sure my aunt and I were safe."

"Okay."

"That's why the moves stopped when my father married and produced a legitimate heir, just like you said before. Anyway, this was less than thirty-five years ago. Poletier might very well be alive and kicking. I'll call this number and see if there's something he can tell me about Leo. If these people are behind Leo's abduction, wouldn't he know?"

"But if Poletier was still alive, wouldn't he have called your aunt and warned her when the prince died?"

"Not if she cut all ties when she moved to Spokane. Who would expect a seventeen-year-old kid to kill himself snowboarding? I bet she thought I was in the clear and let all this craziness go."

"Except she still took precautions. The code for the address book that led to this box, for instance. Your phony up-to-date passport. The emergency money—"

"Ingrained habit? It doesn't matter. It's all I can think to do," he admitted. "If Poletier comes up empty, then it's back to Seattle and legal channels and that will take forever. Montivitz must be about twelve hours ahead of us so it's early afternoon there. May I use your cell phone?"

"Of course," she said, getting to her feet to retrieve the phone from her shoulder bag.

If Leo wasn't in Montivitz, what would they do next?

It didn't pay to think too far ahead.

Chapter Seven

Minister Poletier, it turned out, still lived in the same house he'd lived in over three decades before. Even better, he spoke English, which became clear when, in response to Will's halting French salutation, Poletier demanded to know who was calling him on his private line.

Will spent no time equivocating. He announced his identity which was met with a sharp intake of breath. "William Wellspring," he repeated into the ensuing silence. "You knew my aunt, Fiona Wellspring."

More silence before Poletier said, "How did you get this number?"

"Fiona Wellspring was my aunt," Will repeated. "I found your phone number in an old letter."

"*Was* your aunt?"

"She's dead, Minister Poletier. Under suspicious circumstances. But what's more important at this moment is the fate of my son."

There was a long pause.

"Minister?"

"I don't understand," Poletier said. "Your son?"

"My ten-month-old son, Leonardo Chastain. He's been kidnapped. In fact, many suspicious things have happened to my family since the death of King Lévesque's youngest son. Deaths, kidnappings—the list goes on. Do you have any knowledge of what's happened to Leo?"

"This is terrible news," Poletier said, his voice shaky. "Your child…abducted?"

"Yes."

Another pause, as though every word was measured, every thought examined. "I take it you… know…your…true identity?"

"Yes. But my son—"

"When did he go…missing?"

"A day and a half ago."

"I have…I have no knowledge of your son. I cannot help you."

"Don't hang up," Will said. He steadied his breathing. Poletier's pauses struck him as ominous. "Tell me what you know," he demanded.

"It is nothing."

"Minister? Do you have children? Can you imagine how frantic I am?"

The next pause lasted an eon. "I have a son, yes." Another interminable pause was followed by more halting words. "Yesterday a palace official and his wife adopted an infant."

"A boy?" Will asked, the beating of his heart suspended.

"Yes, yes, but I have seen the papers. This man resides in the castle, most respected, papers in order. The child is from an orphanage on the northern coast. He's almost a year old. He could not be your son."

What was to keep a kidnapper from using a phony birth date? Leo was big for his age, robust and healthy. He could easily pass for a year. And who else would have the means to forge the necessary documents? He'd thought his aunt, but that wasn't the case, he was sure of that now. There was a way to be certain. He said, "Have you seen this baby, Minister Poletier?"

"No. There will be a celebration tonight, but until then—"

"Look at his neck. Leo has a small birthmark on the back of his neck. His mother said it looked like a strawberry. We made jokes because his hair has a reddish glow, like a berry. His eyes are brilliant blue. He can't walk, but he can sit up and crawl. Make an excuse to see the back of this child's neck."

"I don't know—"

"Minister Poletier? Get this straight. I am not going to go away. I'll raise hell in every diplomatic avenue I can find. I'll spread my name and identity across every rumor-hungry scandal sheet, besmirch your king and your country, do whatever I have to do to find and reclaim my son. My father may have turned his back on his son. My aunt may have run scared. I will do neither. I suggest you look at this baby's neck. I'll call you back in eight hours."

"Tell me how to reach you," the minister said. "Tell me where you are."

"No. I'll call you back."

Will flipped off Julia's phone and glanced at her. She sat erect in the chair, hands in her lap, eyes wide and dark. She was holding a folded piece of paper.

"What's that?"

She shook her head as she dropped the paper into her handbag. "Nothing. Did you learn anything new from Minister Poltier?"

He set the phone next to the television. Reaching down, he took her hands in his and pulled her to her feet.

A man could get lost in those chocolate eyes. He raised a hand and brushed hair still damp from the shower away from her forehead. She'd left it down and it floated around her shoulders. "I think so."

"But will Minister Poletier tell you even if he checks and it is Leo?"

"I don't know. I doubt it."

"But—"

His gaze drifted down to her lips.

"I'm scared," she whispered.

"I know." What he wanted to do was kiss away her fear.

"When I think of that baby in a strange place with a stranger taking care of him—"

"If he's there he's in no immediate danger."

"You don't understand," she said, her eyes filling with tears. "At first when Nicole left him with me, he was frightened. He wouldn't sleep. He wasn't sure enough of me to sleep. He'd just sit there in my arms staring at me, trying to keep his eyes open, worried. A little frown, so serious, so precious. I...I knew how he felt. I never pushed him. And then I noticed he stopped crying when Nicole left him and started crying when she took him away. When I think of him with these kidnappers—"

"But if he's there he's alive," Will said, putting it in basic terms. He himself felt re-invigorated by his conversation with Poletier. He was certain Leo was in Monti-vitz and if a high-ranking castle official had announced the child as his own, he wouldn't harm him. "We'll make it okay for Leo when we get him back," he told her.

He realized at once that he'd used a plural pronoun because of the way her eyes sparkled.

The way she trembled in his arms.

"There's nothing we can do from this Canadian motel room in the middle of the night," he added. "If Leo is in Montivitz, if someone has gone to all the trouble of pre-tending to adopt him, then he's safe for the moment. Remember that."

She closed her eyes.

"You're exhausted," he said as his fingers brushed her petal-soft cheek. She leaned into his hand.

Tomorrow, he'd go to Montivitz no matter what Poletier said on the phone. The man sounded timid. Not a powerhouse. Poletier would say whatever was politically expedient to say. Tomorrow, Will would find a safe place to stash Julia while he was gone. He wouldn't endanger her again. He'd steal away when she wasn't looking if he had to.

But that was tomorrow. Tonight, he was here with her, and for once, her defenses seemed down. No doubt she was too tired to resist.

A gentleman would let her be, let her sleep, respect her fatigue.

"I'm no gentleman," he whispered.

She covered a yawn with her hand then said, "What? I'm sorry, I didn't hear you. I'm so tired my head hurts."

She hadn't slept the night before. She'd piloted the plane while he'd drowsed. Who knew what the next day held? Who knew what she'd have to face by herself once he was on his way?

He wanted to sweep her up in his arms and take advantage of her fatigue and her emotional fragility. Gallant? No. He kissed her forehead instead.

"Let's hit the sack," he said.

She sat down on the edge of the sagging mattress, smothering another yawn. He removed his aunt's old box and folded back the blankets, standing aside as Julia all but melted into the sheets, her eyes closing as soon as her head hit the pillow, dark hair fanning across the white linen. Raising the blanket over her prone form, he covered her hips, the gentle swell of her breasts, taking a deep breath as she all but disappeared into a cotton cocoon, out of sight, safe from him.

Dimming the lights, he stepped out of his jeans and got into his own side of the bed, expecting to lie awake for hours while his body cooled down from wanting her and his mind slowed down from worrying about Leo.

Instead he fell into a dreamless sleep.

WILL WOKE UP to find the bed next to him empty, the covers askew as though Julia had had a tough night. He'd been so dead to the world he hadn't even felt her flinch, which didn't do much to reassure him about his keen instincts.

The door to the room opened almost at once and Julia entered, sunshine behind her, breath condensing, cheeks ruddy, hair back in her ponytail.

She looked the picture of contentment but for the anxiety flickering in her eyes. "Good, you're awake," she said. "I bought coffee and rolls—you have to call Poletier in a few minutes."

"Morning," he grumbled, pulling on his jeans. He retreated to the bathroom and closed the door, peering at his face in the mirror before brushing his teeth with the supplies he'd bought at the grocery store the night before. He hadn't thought to buy a razor, so the stubble was going to have to stay.

He put his shirt on and his shoes, then re-entered the room and accepted a steaming cup of coffee. "I might live," he said.

They both turned to stare at the bedside clock. Julia handed Will her phone, but before he flipped it open, she said, "I called George Abbot again this morning. I got to worrying about a ransom call. I mean, my phone was blown up. He said that the police have a tap on the line so if anyone tries to call—"

"No one will call," Will said as he set the half-finished coffee aside.

"But they've connected me to you and now at least one person in Montivitz knows you aren't dead," she said.

He grunted at that remark, and punched in Poletier's number. As he waited for the connection, he met Julia's gaze. Her nervousness leaped across the room and attacked him right as Poletier picked up the phone.

"Listen here, Poletier," he began without giving the older man a chance to say anything more than hello. "I don't want any equivocating from you. I don't believe in coincidences, so before you give me some lame story about how this man and his wife all of a sudden decided to adopt a baby boy the same age as mine—"

"Mr. Wellspring," Poletier interrupted. "Please, sir, I'm trying to tell you. The child is your son."

Will said, "What?"

"The mark on the baby's neck is just as you said it would be."

"Oh, my God. This is wonderful—"

"No, sir, this is terrible."

Will picked up a pencil and paper. "What airline flies into Port Jewel?" Will gave Julia a thumbs-up sign. She buried her face in her hands.

He turned his attention back to the phone where Poletier sputtered, "No, no, you mustn't come here. Never. Much too dangerous. I will start an investigation on this end—"

"No," Will said.

A long pause was followed by cautious words. "You understand that with the death of Prince Federico, you are next in line for the throne of Montivitz?"

"I don't care about the throne," Will said.

"My country is in…flux. There is a rebel here, a man by the name of Paul Bernard, who will stop at nothing to destroy the crown. You arriving on our shores at such a time would be…inflammatory. Unless you aim to claim the throne for yourself—"

"I don't care about becoming king of Montivitz or anywhere else in the world," Will snapped. "My concern begins and ends with Leo."

"But it is not just about you," Poletier said.

"I won't come using the name Wellspring. I have an alias—"

"Your past names are known, sir. Any one of them will be flagged by customs. I urge you not to act rashly. There are diplomatic ways to go about the return of your boy."

In that moment, Will understood that Poletier would never sanction him going to Montivitz. Poletier was too cautious, too loyal to king and country, too afraid to make waves.

But waves had already been made, and if he thought Will was going to sit by and let those waves wash his baby away with the tide, he was mistaken.

However, Will could be diplomatic, too. Maybe it ran in the family. Maybe there was a little king-like material in his DNA. He said, "Perhaps you are right, Minister. Perhaps I should give you a week or so to clear this up."

The man's relief was palpable, even over the phone. "That's very wise of you, very wise indeed. I admire your level head. If you will tell me how to contact you—"

"No, I'll contact you," Will said. "In a few days."

Another pause. "I see. As you like it then. But remember, if things are as you say, you are in great danger."

"I'll watch out for me. You figure out a way to get Leo home. One week, Minister."

He closed the phone and took a look at Julia who appeared horror-struck. She jumped to her feet and faced him, fists white-knuckled. "How could you agree to such a thing? How could you let them keep

Leo for another hour, let alone another week? There has to be a way to get him back sooner. I'll go to Montivitz if you won't."

"And storm the castle?"

"If I have to," she said, and the rage burning in her eyes convinced him she was serious.

He relented. "I'm not going to give him a week, Julia. I'm not going to give him a day. I'll catch the first plane out of here anywhere close to Montivitz and figure out a way to get to the island without being stopped once I get there."

She was gathering up her belongings, stuffing them in her oversized bag. "Good, good," she said. "All those countries you named last night. There has to be a jet going to one of them with a couple of empty seats."

He came up behind her and turned her to face him. "No," he said. "I'm going alone. This is too dangerous. I won't risk you."

She stared at him in such a way that he felt her pain all the way deep into his soul. He'd just betrayed her. He could see it in her eyes, feel it emanating from her body. "I am not yours to risk, William Wellspring."

He winced at the name. He'd been Will Chastain for so many years now, he'd put all the other identities behind him and now here he was again, back where he started. *Thanks, Dad…*

"I don't need you," he said.

The spasm of pain that crossed her face almost undid him.

"I'm not going for *you,*" she told him. "I'm going for *Leo—*"

"He's *my* son." He wanted her so hurt she'd back away and leave him to do what he had to do. But this was like punching someone who refused to fall to the ground.

She said, "Legally, Leo Chastain is *my* son. You're dead, remember?"

"But you have no money to buy a ticket."

"I have plastic. I'll get to wherever Leo is on my own. No one in Montivitz is looking for me. I'll waltz off a nice big jet while you're still paddling across the Mediterranean Ocean in an inner tube."

"What do you mean, no one is looking for you? How about the cops? And if not them, how about the guy who shot your tire, tried to run you down and shoot you and don't forget—blew up your house? How about him?"

"I am not your concern!"

Before he could think of another insult to

throw at her, there was a thump on the wall and a muffled voice yelled, "Will you two knock it off? I'm trying to get some sleep over here!"

He hadn't realized their voices had risen.

He looked into her eyes and opened his mouth to say something, anything that would dissuade her. "That stubborn streak of yours is going to get you killed one of these days."

"Better all dead than half-dead," she said.

He was man enough to know he'd lost.

THE NEAREST international airport was in Vancouver, Canada. It took hours to drive there though Julia thought if she were behind the wheel they'd make better time. She took out her anxiety on the road map, issuing orders like a general.

They made several stops before reaching the airport. One at a chart shop where Will had pored over sea charts of the Mediterranean, purchasing two or three and carrying them in a plastic tube. They'd also stopped at a bookstore and picked up a guide to France and a very small book about Montivitz. The next-to-last stop was at a big discount center where they bought luggage and a few changes of clothes, figuring they might not have another chance to buy the essentials. Plus, getting on board an international flight without luggage seemed a sure way to peg someone's interest and that was the last thing they wanted.

The last stop was the bank where Will checked the balance on the bank card his aunt had set up for him under the name William Noble. He'd come back to the car looking stunned.

"Between checking and savings there's almost a million dollars in that account," he said as he slid behind the wheel.

She'd stayed in the car perusing the Montivitz guidebook while he went into the bank. The island might be small, but the two-thirds not dominated by the American airbase appeared picture-perfect, Port Jewel being the literal jewel of the realm. Cobblestone streets surrounded by charming villas and ritzy stores, views of the sea around every corner, yachts in every inlet and bay. There was a picture of the palace, as well. A castle with turrets and spires, the whole nine yards.

There was also a section on the monarchy. The pictures of the aging king and his handsome son, Federico, still alive and well at that printing, had touched her heart. The prince had looked a lot like Will, same smile, same bone structure. The prince had loved to ski, loved to sail, was photographed with half a dozen young women. It was hard to believe so much vitality was gone forever.

It was hinted that the king collected a lot of taxes and Julia wondered if this had fueled the current dissension in the ranks. Nevertheless, as King Lévesque's son, Will was entitled to more money than he would ever need. A million was just a drop in the bucket.

But she didn't say anything because he'd said so little about his newfound identity. It was obvious his thoughts seldom strayed far from his ultimate goal: reclaim Leo. She'd had some nerve suggesting he keep his focus.

The only available seats on the plane had been in first class. It was the first time Julia had ever ridden on a commercial plane in such luxury. She sat back in the leather chair and closed her eyes, planning on a nice long nap.

But sleep proved as elusive here as it had been in the motel the night before when she'd awakened after an hour to find herself tucked in next to Will. All the feelings she had for him had settled in her stomach as though she'd swallowed a big rock. She'd lain there forever, wishing she could shut off her mind, too aware of his breathing and the heat of his body, trapped because there was nowhere else to go.

So she'd turned over on her side and watched the digital bedside clock flash the hours away, trying not to think about Will, trying not to think about Leo, failing at both tasks. She'd greeted the morning sun as a savior.

And now the words she'd spoken to stop Will's insistence that she stay behind echoed in her ears.

Half-dead.

Is that what she'd been for the past several years?

No, she decided. She'd bought her house and furnished it. She'd taken flying lessons and excelled at them. She'd gotten herself a job, made friends and had a brief platonic relationship with her boss. And she'd tried to befriend Nicole and when it became obvious Nicole was using her as a glorified babysitter, she'd kept her head because she wanted to maintain a relationship with Nicole's baby. Nicole's very precious baby.

That was living, right?

Okay, it was all kind of safe. With the exception of giving her heart to Leo, she'd avoided emotional entanglements. Other than George, she hadn't dated. She got high on piloting and relaxed by turning the key in her front door. What was wrong with any of that?

A more pertinent question stuck up its hand and demanded attention. What should she do about the letter she'd found the night before? She'd found it on the floor when she got up to get the phone for Will, and now it lurked in her purse like a poison dart. If she told Will, what would his reaction be? Did knowing what the letter said change anything about what they were planning on doing? And what *were* they planning to do? If Will had a master scheme in mind, he was keeping it to himself.

Her thoughts were once again spiraling into neverending circles and she sighed. She'd keep the contents of the letter to herself for now. She'd wait.

Will waved away an offer of champagne. Julia shook her head as well. One glass of the stuff would knock her out for good. Wait a second—maybe that's what she needed.

"Lots of time now to get to know each other," Will said. "This is a fourteen-hour flight."

Fourteen hours. Good Lord.

"Nicole told me you were an orphan," he said.

Was this how he intended on passing the next fourteen hours? Yikes. She was not up to this discussion. She said, "We need magazines. And that champagne. I changed my mind. Where's the flight attendant?"

"Julia?"

"What?"

"Stop fidgeting. Talk to me."

She stopped searching the aisle and met his gaze. "You're an architect. What do you design?"

He looked surprised by her question. Ah-ha. He'd intended this show-and-tell to be about her, not him. He smiled and said, "Right before I 'died,' I was working on an upscale housing community built around a small lake. Houses clustered together, infrastructure all in place. You know, restaurants, stores, all that close by, a community center, public square, a real village feel."

"Sounds quaint."

"It was turning out pretty retro," he said, a quick frown creasing his brow. "I wonder how it's getting along without me."

"When this is over, will you go back?"

"I don't know," he said. "I can't picture this ever being over. How about you?"

"When this is over? I'll take my fire insurance money and rebuild my house," she said. "I'll go back to work."

He looked contemplative. They'd both sunk down in their seats, and she wondered if she could close her eyes and rest. She was giving it a test drive when he asked another question.

"I want to know about you, Julia. If I remember this right, Nicole's mother and your mother were half sisters."

Here it comes, she thought. Opening her eyes, she turned her head to look at him, intending to beg fatigue. But his earnest expression shamed her into answering. "My last foster mother searched on the Internet until she found Nicole's mother and that's how I connected with Nicole."

"Nicole's mother lives in upstate New York, on a farm with her third husband. Too rural for Nicole. I guess her mother and her butted heads all of Nicole's life. I was expecting they'd get close again when Leo was born, but the mother has kind of adopted her husband's kids as her own and didn't care much about our baby."

Julia shook her head. "Aren't people amazing? The way we...squander...each other."

He squeezed her hand. "Nicole wouldn't tell me what happened to your family, Julia. She said her mother wouldn't talk about it and you wouldn't either."

"And you want to know," Julia said.

"Yes."

"Why?"

"Because you know all about my crazy family and I know nothing about you except what Nicole told me."

"Which is?"

"That your sister and parents died in the same year, that you went to live with your grandmother but she got sick and that's when you went into the foster-care system. Nicole's mother could have stepped in to help but she didn't."

"My grandmother was no relation at all to Nicole's mother."

"But you—"

She shook her head. "Don't. Nicole's mother didn't offer. The courts asked her, but she didn't want another child. Nicole was only a couple of years older than me. The poor woman no doubt had her hands full. She didn't need another girl."

He started to say something, but she narrowed her eyes. How could she bear to have this discussion with him if he was going to second-guess decisions made a lifetime ago? Decisions she'd no power to control. Had she spent most of her life wishing this distant aunt had rescued her? Of course. Was it one of the main reasons she was so torn up about not being able to rescue Leo? No doubt.

"Tell me what happened to your folks and your sister," he said, laying his head back so that they were almost nose to nose, mouth to mouth.

She closed her eyes, shutting out the fog-gray irises so close to her own, shutting out the stab of desire that assaulted her every time her gaze lingered on his lips.

"Julia?" he whispered.

"My sister was a year older than me," she said. Julia had heard the story once, from her grandmother before she died. She herself had never repeated it out loud. She'd held it close, the tragedy so personal it couldn't be shared with the dozen families whose homes, if not hearts, she'd come in and out of over the years. However, she'd pictured the events in her mind a million times, so that now, on the quiet plane with her eyes closed and her body cosseted by soft leather, with Will's bigger presence shielding her from the rest of the world, she relented. It was like talking about a dream, about something that had happened to someone else.

"Her name was Sara. My grandmother had just a few pictures of her, taken with me when we were both tiny little girls. We looked enough alike to be twins."

The image from that picture flashed behind her eyes. The photograph was in— had been in—with the ones of her grandmother. And her parents. All gone now. Ashes. Like her house. Like her life.

"One summer afternoon when I was about five and Sara six, my mother went to get her hair done at a salon. We didn't have a lot of money so that was a big deal for her. She left me and Sara with my father. I was playing over on the grass and Sara was by my father who was washing his truck. While his attention was on his wheels or something, Sara wandered away. By the time my father looked up, Sara had moved down the driveway into the street, between parked cars. He started toward her, seeing for the first time that she had followed a couple of monarch butterflies as they flitted around each other. She was so preoccupied with them that she didn't respond to his yells."

The butterflies fluttered and dipped through Julia's imagination. Two large orange-and-black lace creatures. The innocent leading the innocent astray.

"Julia?"

She bit her lip. "My father heard a car turn the corner and shouted at Sara to stop. That's all I can remember about this. Everything else is what my grandmother told me. Before Dad could get to her, she stepped from between the parked cars and into the path of the coming automobile."

A shudder ran through Julia's body. Will clutched her arms and she opened her eyes, surprised to find her cheeks damp.

"My God," he said.

"Sara died instantly. After that, everything… changed. Mom started drinking, Dad couldn't concentrate and lost his job at the paper mill, they started fighting. I have a vague recollection of raised voices, but I spent a lot of time at my grandmother's, so who knows, maybe I just think I remember the arguments. Long story short, my mother went off the deep end. In a drunken rage, she shot my father and then herself."

Will drew in his breath.

"My grandmother said my mother couldn't forgive my father for Sara's death. She said my mother went crazy."

"I'd say your grandmother was right," Will said.

"She just couldn't handle the…pain."

Leaning forward, he kissed her lips, drying her tears with his thumbs. "She was a coward, Julia. She took the easy way out. If she'd looked outside her own misery, she would have seen you standing there."

It was on the tip of her tongue to lash out at his condemnation. She should defend her mother from other people. It was one thing for her to admit hurt, but to hear it echoed back was too painful to bear. She should never have spilled her guts.

"I won't ask you to abandon the search for Leo again," he added. "I understand now. It's okay."

The flight attendant arrived, offering

pillows and blankets. Julia took one of each, and feigning sleep, turned her face away.

TOO MUCH SLEEP, Julia thought as they boarded another plane, this one bound for Toulon, a port city on the southern coast of France. From there, Will informed her, they would rent a boat to cross the Mediterranean Sea to the island of Montivitz.

Her head felt heavy, her body logy. She'd slept for ten hours straight and had awoken all catawampus, her face plastered against Will's chest, the imprint of one of his buttons pressed into her cheek. He'd been asleep, too, and for a second, she'd indulged in the fantasy of intimacy. By the time he stirred, however, she'd found a magazine and was adjusting the window shade.

Paris had been a dazzling array of lights. Toulon, approached as the sun rose, was everything Julia's impression of the Côte d'Azur dictated it be. Winding roads, whitewashed buildings that shone golden in the morning sun, hillsides crowned with ancient forts and the sea beyond the harbor a sparkling blue blanket as far as the eye could see.

And somewhere out there, Montivitz, and with any luck, Leo.

Chapter Eight

Will used his classroom French to rent them a car and took over the driving as his ability to read French meant he could decipher road signs. He'd studied the French guide book on the last flight, dog-earing pages that highlighted what he needed, so he knew they should head for the harbor. The traffic on the Quai Stalingrad was horrendous, but he faced it with businesslike concentration. Thanks tò the sleep he got on the plane, he felt well rested and energized.

As Toulon formed France's major naval base, the harbor area was a no-nonsense place. They passed signs advertising harbor and neighboring island tours, looking for the marina that was home to smaller craft and independent boats for hire. He didn't want a crew. He needed a vessel he could handle by himself, as Julia admitted she'd never been on a boat. Something with enough power to cross over a hundred miles of sea without danger, something nondescript enough to arouse no suspicion once they got there.

He hadn't looked at the Montivitz book yet. He'd tried, but the picture of the fairy-tale island on the cover put him off. It looked pretend, like something out of a theme park. Besides, if that blasted island was responsible for destroying the lives of everyone he loved, then he didn't feel very warm and cozy about it.

Beyond rescuing Leo, his main wish concerning Montivitz was a one-on-one with his father. There were questions that needed answers. Plus, his father had to know about the recent mayhem perpetuated right under his nose without his knowledge.

They parked and hurried down a dock that promised a boat rental, bypassing any number of yachts, the more modest ones reminding him of his late great boat. Another couple stood at the small desk inside the dockside office. Will eavesdropped for a moment as they discussed craft and prices with the proprietor, M. B. Giscard, according to the name plate on his desk. He then stepped back outside next to Julia, content to wait in the sunshine and give the people their privacy.

"It's beautiful here," Julia said. She'd produced a pair of sunglasses from her voluminous satchel and taken off her leather jacket. Even in jeans and a turtleneck shirt, she looked right at home.

He took her hand. What would it be like to be here on vacation with her, sightseeing with no cares, ending the evening with a long night of lovemaking, starting the next day with croissants and coffee and no firm plans?

She rested her head on his shoulder as though she shared his fantasy. He felt an alarming desire to make up for the things she'd lost in life. The family, the closeness, the love. Dangerous thoughts, a fool's errand. He could no more "fix" her than she could "fix" him.

But maybe together…

A glimpse of a man in a dark suit stalking down the dock drew Will from his musing. Even though the guy wore dark glasses, it was clear he was looking this way and that, searching for something. Or someone. His behavior and the pasty whiteness of his skin made him stand out like an FBI agent at a kid's pool party.

Will had started to nudge Julia when the man's gaze swerved around and landed on them. For one beat, the guy's step faltered. Within another beat, he'd veered off onto an adjacent dock that jutted out at a right angle. He didn't look back.

"We have to get out of here," Will said, pulling on Julia's hand.

The other couple and the owner had just exited. Julia, caught up in the small gathering, resisted Will's urging. Will looked down the perpendicular dock and caught sight of the man between yachts, his black suit a beacon on the sun-drenched dock. He was staring across boats and water, right at Will.

"Julia. Come on," Will said.

"But Monsieur Giscard says he can talk to us now," she said, turning from the eager face of the proprietor to Will. An iridescent smile lit her eyes.

With one glance at him, the smile disappeared. "Excuse us," she said to Giscard. Asking no questions, she dogged Will's steps away from the office. The man on the next dock started back toward the juncture of the two docks. There was no direction to go but straight ahead, toward the ramp leading into the parking area. "Run," Will said.

They sailed by the juncture a few steps in front of the man in the suit, the pounding of their footsteps drumming in Will's ears. They flew off the dock and into the parking area, skirting cars to get to their rental. They'd almost made it when Julia's hand slipped from his. Will ground to a halt and looked back.

Their pursuer had caught her other hand and yanked her back against him. He was a giant of a man, something Will hadn't registered until that instant. Almost as tall as he was broad, he held Julia in a viselike grip with big, meaty paws. She struggled to get free, raising her shoulder bag and slugging him over the head with it, sending his sunglasses flying, revealing hard blue eyes.

Like brushing away an annoying insect, the man raised a hand and slapped Julia to the ground.

Rage fired Will's dive toward the man's knees. Might as well have attacked a cement pillar. He landed on his stomach. He turned and kicked at the back of the giant's legs. The maneuver felled him like a redwood tree, but he turned out to be as fast as he was big. Within an instant, he'd regained his footing and planted a colossal shoe on Will's chest. He pushed down. A sharp pain signaled a rib cracking.

Smiling now, the thug said something Will couldn't understand.

Will caught a glimpse of Julia, blood streaming down her face from a cut on her cheekbone, flying toward their mugger's back. She jumped him, pummeling with her fists, yelling her outrage.

The man shifted his weight and Will rolled away, escaping that enormous foot, taking advantage of diverted attention to scramble to his own feet, the cracked rib like a knife cutting into his side. By the time he turned to face the action, he found the thug had grabbed Julia's hair and dragged her back against him.

Julia gasped for breath, her bloody face contorted with pain. Will looked around for help. The parking lot was empty.

The man held a gun against Julia's neck. Keeping one arm wrapped around Julia, he waved the gun toward a black van.

As the tip of the gun floated in midair, Will launched himself once again. Julia anticipated his move and wrenched herself free, sacrificing long dark strands of hair caught in the giant's fist, kicking back with her boot at his knee at the same time Will hit the guy mid-chest. With a stroke of luck, the combination of actions knocked him off balance and he fell, landing on his face, the gun firing into his own belly.

Will scrambled to his feet.

The man lay dead, mouth half-open, eyes staring at nothing. The gun had fallen free of his body.

In the still after the storm, Will heard Julia catch a sob. He looked down to find her fingers inching toward the gun.

"Don't touch it," he said.

"But—"

He retrieved her shoulder bag and hauled her to her feet, ignoring the blinding pain in his side. Onlookers had finally begun to gather, drawn no doubt by the sound of gunfire. Julia was shaking so hard her teeth chattered.

He pushed her toward their rental, unlocked her door, urged her inside. In another heartbeat, he slid behind the wheel and backed out of the lot. As he gained the highway, he accelerated, his sole aim to put as much distance between them and the dead man as possible.

"I need help," he said, sparing her a glance. She nodded as she dug in her bag and came up with a packet of hand wipes, one of which she pressed against the gash on her cheekbone.

"First, put your head between your knees," he added, afraid she was about to pass out.

"Can't," she said. "No time." With one hand, she rummaged in the bag for the French guidebook. "We need an alternate location, right?"

"Yes. Somewhere on the coast. Somewhere not too far away."

"Who was that monster?" she said as she thumbed through the guidebook. Her hands shook and he saw her bite her lip.

"I don't have the slightest idea."

"He looked dead."

"Yes."

"Why didn't we take his gun? We don't have a weapon and we might need one."

"I know. But people saw us leave the scene. Neither one of us touched the gun so the police will find just his fingerprints."

"So they might not connect us with murder."

"That's the plan."

A moment or two later, she mumbled, "St. Martinez. It appears to be twenty miles or so away. Maybe less."

"Does it look big enough to have a harbor?"

She read for a moment before muttering, "It looks big enough. But boat rentals aren't mentioned in the book."

"We'll steal a boat if we have to," he said. He spared her a look and added, "Are you okay? That gash on your cheek—"

"I just need a bandage," she said. "How about you? You were holding your side—"

"I think the creep busted one of my ribs. I'll live."

She gave concise directions, and soon they were traveling along a much smaller road that curved inland before swerving toward the sea once again. It was easier to keep a lookout for tailing cars.

They stopped in a copse of pine trees before descending into the town, doing some minor first aid with the help of the small emergency kit Julia carried with the rest of her supplies, then changing out of their clothes. He dressed in khakis and a cream polo shirt, wincing whenever he moved. She donned a long beige skirt and a coral tunic that lent her pale complexion a hint of color. She twisted her hair on top of her head and secured it with a pin, topping the effort with a floppy sun hat; they both exchanged boots for sandals. Confident they didn't look much like the couple last seen fighting with the dead man in Toulon, they got back in the car and drove into the city.

St. Martinez turned out to be a village without Toulon's glitz or its crowds. It was compact enough that all roads seemed to lead to the harbor area. Flowers spilling over the embankment set off a small fleet of fishing vessels and sailboats nestled against picturesque gray docks. Surely something that floated could be borrowed, rented or bought.

Or stolen.

THE BOAT they settled on was the only boat anyone was willing to part with. A big old sixty-foot ketch built of oak three-quarters of a century before, the *Marie Antoinette* seemed to squat in the water rather than float atop it. Julia thought the name an ill omen.

The Frenchman who bargained with Will looked shifty to Julia. She couldn't understand a word he and Will said to each other, only that the man was willing to take American dollars and quite a lot of them. He pointed out to sea, saying an alarming number of things, punctuated with the word, "Montivitz." Julia also heard him say, *"Non, non,"* in answer to Will's halting questions. Her nervous state ratcheted up a few notches.

As soon as they were alone, she expressed her doubts. "The boat is too big for the two of us to handle, or are you forgetting I don't know a thing about sailboats?"

"I haven't forgotten," he said, folding a few Euros he'd conned out of the owner. He stuffed them in his pocket and added, "This guy has only had the boat a few months. Took it in payment of a debt. The previous owner rigged it for solo sailing. It's got everything you'd need to cross an ocean. Trust me, we'll manage."

"And what did he say about Montivitz?"

"He warned us to stay away from it. He's heard trouble is brewing. Malcontents wanting to kick out the Americans, overthrow the monarchy, the usual. Threats of riots. He doesn't want his boat confiscated."

"What did you tell him?"

"I told him it was our honeymoon and we

weren't going anywhere near anyone else. I paid him enough to buy this tub, so we should be okay. Let's get going. Unless you want to stand around here giving the locals something to talk about, something to report to the police should they catch up with us."

They bought groceries and unloaded them and their baggage onto the boat, then drove the car to a lot where they purchased a week's parking. They walked back to the boat, hand in hand, trying their best to appear carefree, just in case anyone was watching.

"I'm wanted for questioning in two countries," she said as they made their way down the dock, both of them fighting the urge to look over their shoulders and dart between piers.

"You've also been on the scene of a shooting, a kidnapping, a hit-and-run, an intruder, a mugging and a couple of suspicious deaths—did I miss anything?"

"You forgot I no longer have a house or a car or much of anything else."

He squeezed her hand. "I haven't forgotten," he said, and climbing aboard the broad-beamed boat, reached down to offer her a hand. Knowing how much his side hurt, she hauled herself aboard.

After wrapping Will's chest in the long elastic bandage they'd bought at a pharmacy, Julia stowed things away. Will retrieved the sea charts from his luggage and spread them out on the table. He spent the better part of an hour studying them as she made cheese sandwiches and coffee. They ate topside then Will began talking to the locals. Julia didn't understand what he said or what questions he asked. She guessed from his hand movements and the direction of everyone's gaze that they were discussing things like tides and currents.

It was almost dark by the time they filled the water and fuel tanks, battened down the hatches—his term—and pulled away from the dock, using the engine. "We'll motor until the wind comes up," Will told her, never taking his eyes from the channel ahead. A sputtering coughing noise erupted just then and he added, "Or until the engine dies. Whichever comes first."

"Reassuring," Julia said, but she smiled when she said it. The truth was that for the first time since facing her most recent attacker, she felt safe. And why not? It was a beautiful clear night with stars overhead and not another boat in sight. Being out on the sea in a boat was akin to being up in the air in an airplane. Both were self-contained capsules in a way, barriers against the void.

Thanks to the ingestion of a couple of aspirin, her cheek had stopped throbbing and the bandages seemed to be holding their own. She knew she'd have a black eye the next day.

"We haven't talked much about the man who attacked us," she said. It was a balmy evening but a shiver still snaked down her spine when the memory of his ruthless power skittered across her mind. She moved closer to Will in the generous cockpit. Perched on the thick wood that surrounded the cockpit, one leg braced on the cockpit floor, the other bent at the knee, foot resting atop a seat, hands on the wheel, his eyes glowed in the subdued light of the instrument panel. He reached out his free hand and pulled her closer.

"What's there to say?" he murmured, his mouth so close to her face that his breath felt warm against her skin.

"True."

He drew back a couple of inches and stared into her eyes. As worried as she was, her heart skipped a beat. "There's no way of knowing who sent him or if he was even connected with Leo's disappearance. Did he follow us or was he waiting for us? No answers."

Julia had spent most of her childhood being pushed around by people but at least none of them had tried to kill her. She'd been groped, slapped, yelled at and punished for things she didn't do. But no one had ever shot at her, no one had tried to run her over or blown up her belongings. She'd thought she'd built up a thick skin, she'd thought she was tough and now she found she was as fragile as the walls that had once formed her home. Walls that were rubble now. And without her facade, without her safe place to return to, who was she, where would she go?

She was a walking target.

I am not a target. I worked hard to be strong and I will stay strong. I can still fly a plane and that's where I've felt the most secure. That's what I'll return to.

He pulled her even closer so that she leaned against him, her hips between his legs. Her skirt fluttered around her calves. She put her arms around his torso, aware of the thick bandage under his shirt. For a second, she felt safe. It was an illusion, of course. In many ways, Will presented the biggest danger of all.

"Why do you do that?" he asked, his lips against her forehead, his beard scratchy against her skin.

"Do what?"

"Come close and then pull away," he said.

She stopped herself from pulling away and said, "I don't—"

"One minute you're the most alluring woman I've ever met. One minute, you feel like you could be mine. It drives me crazy. But then you switch off, you draw back, you go somewhere else. Why?"

"I didn't know I did that," she whispered, but it was a lie. Of course she knew. She'd always done that with men. They were bigger, they liked power; a woman had to be cautious. The memory of a talk very similar to this between herself and George Abbot well over a year before surfaced in her mind. With George she'd been relieved he'd sensed her withdrawal and set her free, that he'd had the guts to do what she couldn't.

But Will was different.

"I don't know what to say," she mumbled.

"Has some man…hurt you?" he asked.

"You mean sexually?"

"Yes."

"One of my foster fathers grabbed me when I was about thirteen," she said. This event was something else she'd never talked about, seldom even thought about. In a blinding moment of insight, she realized she'd kept secrets in an attempt to protect herself. But it hadn't protected her, it had alienated her from herself, from the facts of her life, from understanding who she was and why.

Great time for introspection.

"Did he hurt you?"

"He tried. He pushed me down on the bed, tore my clothes, pawed at me. The usual."

"In what world is that 'the usual'?"

"In mine. He was a big man, like the guy today. He smelled like stale beer and staler cigarettes. First chance I got, I bit his ear so he hauled back and slugged me."

"Just like the guy today," he said, his fingers grazing her cheek.

"Except for the biting part. Anyway, who knows what would have happened next if his wife hadn't walked in. I was ushered out that very afternoon."

"I'd like to find him and beat him to a pulp."

She smiled. "No one has ever wanted to beat someone to a pulp on my behalf."

"Do you find it sexy?"

"Yeah, I think I do."

"Good. So, just the one man—"

"Oh, you know, there were always boys around. Some were the natural children of the different families I lived with, some were foster kids like me. Some of them liked to push girls around. Some of them tried things."

"But you escaped?"

"I escaped. I escaped rape, alcohol, drugs, promiscuity. I was lucky."

"You were strong," he said.

"I had to be. When you're miserable, all those avenues can seem very appealing. Ways to numb yourself. But in the end, I think I became too wary."

He sighed deeply. "Then you're just not interested in me that way," he said.

"That's not true," she blurted out.

"Then don't pull away," he said. After a glance at the compass and a turn of the wheel to correct their course, he tied off the helm with a few economic moves and stared at her, his eyes dark and unfathomable.

It was up to her to make the next move.

What was needed was a leap of faith.

She stared into his eyes. Calm gray eyes like a still pond. Cheeks covered with a day or two worth of beard, obscuring the remnants of the burns. His steady gaze presented an invitation, not a challenge. She was welcome to join him or not, the choice was hers.

She raised a hand and touched his cheek. And leapt.

This time as his kisses grew more and more demanding, she ignored the voices in her head urging caution, ignored her fear, didn't care if they sailed off the end of the world and fell into a giant abyss. This time she opened her heart and shut her mind.

One of his hands cupped her bottom, then slid down her skirt and back up one of her bare legs, his fingers hot against her thigh. She felt herself pulsing with desire for him, yearning for his fingers to touch her, to tear away her underwear, to quench the building fire that throbbed in her the way the boat engines throbbed beneath their feet.

His kisses trailed down her neck, her blouse was soon unbuttoned and he kissed the top curve of her breasts above her bra, drew his fingers over her satin-covered nipples. She arched in closer to him. She'd never wanted a man like this, never felt this wild abandon, never wished he would go further, go faster. She pulled at his shirt, aching to press her bare breasts against his chest.

What about the rib? What about the bandage?

This time, he pulled away from her.

"What's wrong?" she gasped. "Did I hurt you?"

"Never. It's the engine," he said.

"The engine?"

"Listen. It's making a new noise."

She heard the same racket she'd heard before. "You can kiss me like that and still listen to an engine?"

"I'm a good multitasker," he said with a smile that flashed white teeth. "No, honey, listen."

It wasn't necessary for her to listen because in the next moment, the engine gave a final sputter and died.

There still wasn't enough wind to raise the sails, Will said, swearing at fickle machines and dead calm. He kicked the compass stand for good measure, swearing again when the gesture jarred his rib.

Julia caught his hand. "Rotten luck," she said.

"Yeah, well, that's the way it goes. It's not like I've never been becalmed before. The wind will come up, we just have to wait."

"How shall we pass the time?" she mused. "Hmm—"

He gathered her in his arms. "We could study the guidebook of Montivitz to make sure we know where to land and how to get to Port Jewel."

She ran a hand down his cheek, along his jawline, traveled the contour of his ear with a fingertip. "I already did that," she whispered. "I'll tell you about it later. What I was wondering was if you have any kind of protection, because you started something a few moments ago and I think it's time for you to finish it."

"I believe it was you who started something," he countered, the old smile back on his face. "And I do have protection, down below. Wait here and I'll get it."

He disappeared inside. The cabin light flashed on. Julia heard noises, then the light went off and he reappeared, bracing himself against the gentle rolling motion of the hull.

He'd brought blankets and pillows as well as a handful of foil packets.

"Should I ask why you happen to carry around condoms?" she asked. He was making them a bed in the cockpit, layering blankets, fluffing pillows, staring at her as he worked, eyes dark hollows, but glittering hollows that pierced right through her. In alternate waves, she pulsed with anticipation and shook with nerves.

"I bought them in Canada when I went to the store for food that second night," he said.

"You take a lot for granted."

He fell to his knees and tugged on her hands. "I take nothing for granted, not with you," he said. "More like wishful thinking." He slipped her still-unbuttoned blouse from her shoulders; his eyes shone as he gazed at her. "Do you have any idea how gorgeous you are?"

"I'm not—"

"Shh." Reaching up, he pulled the pin from her hair and spread his fingers through the thick mass, kissing her throat. "Where were we?" he asked, his voice huskier than she'd ever heard it.

"Your rib—"

"To hell with my rib."

The moon had risen higher in the sky, casting soft light earthward, a golden glow cascading over their bodies as they undressed one another. Julia was stunned by the look of a naked and aroused male. She'd never made love. Oh, she knew the logistics, the physicality of the act. She wasn't a recluse. She watched movies, she read books; sex was everywhere. But she'd never gone this far with a man before. She'd never allowed herself to let it go this far.

Nerves resurfaced.

"You're trembling," he said.

She didn't trust her voice to answer.

His kisses trailed down her breasts, down her belly, his fingers gripping her derriere. She was engulfed in flames. The fear was supplanted by molten desire, so hot and so needy that grasping his head, she pulled his face back to hers and kissed him, wanting to engulf and be engulfed, needing to lose herself inside him.

He lifted her and she positioned her body astride his, wrapping her legs around him, gasping at the first feel of penetration. He paused and their eyes met, but she pulled him closer, existing only in that one moment, crying out at his renewed thrusts, first with pain then with rapture until he exploded inside her and she rode a wave of euphoria back to earth.

"Julia," he whispered, kissing her forehead, her eyelids, her throat. "You didn't tell me this was your first time. I didn't know—"

But her body had started to respond to his again. She lay back on the blanket and crooked her finger.

Who knew she could be such a wanton hussy?

The time for conversation would come later.

Much later.

THE WIND came up, giving the impression they'd summoned it from the depths of their passion.

Julia pulled on underpants and her tunic, forgoing her skirt as too cumbersome. Will pulled on jeans and nothing else except for the ever-present bandage wrapping his muscular chest. Following his directions, she steered the boat according to the compass as he moved over the moonlit decks like a silent wraith, unfurling sails and hoisting them up the masts. They appeared as wispy ghosts until Will took the wheel and, adjusting the helm, filled them with the breath of life, turning them into the wings of angels.

It was a magical night, though the undercurrent of tension over what they would find in Montivitz was never far away. Will resumed his position behind the wheel, and Julia, wrapped in one of the blankets, sat on the cockpit seat between his legs, her head against his chest, one arm draped over his bent thigh, the warm breeze blowing in her face, tangling her loose hair. She fell in and out of sleep, half awakening, then realizing where she was, on whom she rested, and descending again into slumber.

She awoke for the last time that morning with the sun and watched the water turn from gray to blue and the distant island grow larger.

"Take the helm, keep her on this heading," Will said after kissing her good morning. "I need to check charts."

Julia, left alone in the cockpit, studied the approaching island with interest. She'd read it was three hundred square miles, flat on one side where the Americans had built their air base and where the island had its own airstrip, cliffs on the other side plunging to the sea below. Population less than a million, Port Jewel not only the capital but the major harbor.

Were they just going to sail into Port Jewel and tie up to a visitor dock like a regular tourist? What then? Demand some unknown palace official relinquish Leo? With Nicole dead and Will's life in ruins, did proof of Leo's true identity still exist? Proof that would hold up in a court without the delay of a DNA test? And might not the king just refuse to allow a well-documented adopted child to be taken away from his current family?

The king! She'd forgotten about the letter she'd found, the one she'd secreted away instead of showing to Will. How could she have forgotten such a thing?

A smile curved her lips. The answer was obvious. She'd been so caught up in the thrill of her sexual awakening that she'd let all other thoughts slide from her head.

For the first time, she allowed herself to consider the details of the coming hours. Fear fluttered in her chest like a trapped animal. Once again she had the feeling she'd had before: Will would need her help before the end, Leo would depend on her.

Would she be up to the task? Would she fail both of them?

Will came back into the cockpit, folded chart in hand, looking so capable and sure of himself that her fears should have wafted away like smoke in the wind.

Instead they tripled, they quadrupled as something very primal, something very oblique but persistent, whispered in her ear.

She would lose him on this island.

Chapter Nine

Will looked from the view of the island off the port bow to his wristwatch and then at Julia. "Is something wrong?"

"I have to talk to you," she said, standing. "Take the wheel, I have to get something downstairs."

"I don't like the look on your face," he said as she passed him. She was back in a few moments, holding a piece of paper against her chest.

Her eyes looked everywhere but at him. His first thought was that she regretted their lovemaking. He let that go. He'd bet big money she didn't regret a moment of it. He knew he didn't.

"It's a letter," she said, sitting by his side. She'd pulled on three-quarter-length baggy cotton pants. Pity. On the other hand, her long bare legs had presented quite a distraction. Her hair still framed her face though, fanning out all around her as the wind blew. She looked so beautiful that his heart stopped for a moment and a rush of feelings flooded his head. He kissed her forehead and made himself concentrate.

"What's this?" he asked, taking the letter.

"I found it the night before last. It came from your aunt's box, along with the photographs of your family, before we knew for sure that Leo was on Montivitz. It was all by itself without an envelope. I found it on the floor. I thought that maybe you wouldn't have to see it. That if Leo weren't here, it could be forgotten…"

Her voice trailed off and a sick feeling grew in his gut. He unfolded the paper.

Short, to the point.

You hereby have it upon my authority to use whatever means necessary to eliminate the threat to the monarchy of Montivitz posed by Fiona Ellen Wellspring and her nephew, William Steven Wellspring, both of Chicago, Illinois, America.

Theodore Lévesque

The words were overlaid with a faded but official-looking red imprint of a crown surrounded by an intricate wreath of leaves and berries and dated the year Will was born.

His father had wanted him dead. All these years of hoping and praying his father would come for him, only to find the past upheavals, to say nothing of the recent chaos, were dictated and sanctified not by some radical extremists, but by him.

Will refolded the paper and stuck it in his jeans pocket.

"It must have come in with a letter from Poletier," Julia said.

Will corrected the compass course. He nodded.

"I'm sorry I kept it from you. I hoped that you wouldn't have to see it. Then last night I forgot—"

He drew her close, his hand tangled in her hair. "It's not your fault," he said.

"I can't imagine how you feel."

Couldn't she? Her mother had chosen death over sticking it out and being there for her surviving daughter. She'd even eliminated Julia's father. Will thought it possible Julia knew very well how he felt. He leaned over and kissed her, liking her all the more because she was so damn decent.

Liking her? Was it too soon to admit that his feelings amounted to a whole lot more than that?

He met her gaze. She'd come a long way last night. She'd trusted him—a huge step. He wouldn't push her; he'd be patient.

Besides, he was a marked man and a marked man had no right falling in love with anyone, let alone someone who had already lost so much.

"The letter doesn't change a thing," he said, bringing the boat into the wind. Standing, he lowered the small mizzen sail in preparation for standing offshore until dark. The island was getting too close, though he doubted the waters were patrolled. He could see other boats in the distance and imagined a thriving trade of tourists and boaters existed between France, Italy and Montivitz.

"What are we doing?" she asked, looking into his eyes.

He finished furling the aft sail and brought the boat around again to stop the flapping of the main sail while they talked. "We're going to bypass Port Jewel and head for a little cove around the southeast point. The charts show a shallow bottom and a sandy beach. We'll row ashore and take an overland route to Port Jewel."

"What about customs?"

"No customs. We'll anchor the boat tonight after dark, as far away from shore as possible and without running lights. We'll row ashore. It's only a couple of miles to the castle. We'll walk there if we have to and rescue Leo. We'll bring him back here and take him home."

She stared at him as though he were crazy, and despite everything, he grinned. "Bring the boat back into the wind while I lower the mainsail, Julia."

"What does that mean?"

"Point it into the wind until the boat stops moving forward and the sail flaps around. And don't worry, I'll finesse the plan as we go along."

"I hope so," she said.

"You're forgetting about our ace in the hole, good old Minister Poletier."

"You think he'll help us?"

"If it comes down to helping us or being a part of disgracing country and king, yeah, I do."

"Or maybe you could threaten to move to Montivitz and claim the crown."

He laughed out loud. "I will if I have to," he said.

SINCE JULIA had slept on and off during the night, the first watch was left to her. The old hulk swayed on the mild swells as Julia sat in the cockpit, staring at the island, aware of a rattling can under a cockpit seat that rolled back and forth with the boat. It took her forever to dig out and secure the empty can of an engine additive and stop the annoying rattle.

The island looked so peaceful as the sun shone down on its bluffs and beaches. Hard to believe unrest bubbled and brewed in such an exotic setting.

Will awoke after five or six hours and sent Julia to the bunk for her turn. Despite her nerves, she fell asleep at once, lulled by the motion, comforted by a sleeping bag still warm from Will's body.

She was walking in the sun. A man took her hand. She turned. An eight-foot ogre leered down at her. She screamed. He opened his mouth. A fountain of red erupted, gushing like a waterfall, spilling around her feet, washing up her legs. The ogre turned into Will. His hand slipped from hers as he sank into a lake of churning red blood—

She sat up, banging her head against the low bulkhead, her heart pounding in her chest.

She closed her eyes and took a deep breath, rubbing her forehead with her fingers. She was on the *Marie Antoinette,* and it wasn't rolling anymore.

Did this awful dream fit in with the premonition she couldn't shake? What was with this psychic hocus-pocus all of a sudden? What she needed was a strong cup of coffee and a swift kick in her behind.

She took a moment to dress in jeans and a black cotton sweater before going up on deck.

"Evening," Will said, smiling at her.

Sometime during the day, he'd shaved and changed into jeans and dark T-shirt. With the ocean at his back and the white sails filled with wind billowing over his head, he appeared to be in his natural element.

"Come here," he said, holding out a hand. She crossed the cockpit and tucked herself against him.

"Did you get some sleep? I was down

there a while ago heating soup and you seemed restless."

"I'm fine," she said, but the truth was that her heart had lodged somewhere in her throat while a gallon or two of battery acid sloshed in her stomach. She kissed his neck and wished—

Wished what? If none of this had ever happened, she would never have met him, except for perhaps sometime in the future as Nicole's detested ex. Okay, she wished it was over. She couldn't get rid of the dread that seemed to be creeping over her heart like black spot on a rose leaf. She took a long look at the island.

It now filled the whole horizon. Buildings clinging to the mountainsides could be seen along with automobile lights winding down twisting roads. Lights from other seacraft were visible to the west around the harbor at Port Jewel.

"You're developing quite a shiner," Will said. Julia knew it. She'd applied new bandages and seen the purple bruising under her eye.

"Makes me look mysterious," she said.

"Hmm… Well, I found a weapon while you slept." Reaching into his pocket, he withdrew an orange handgun, but it was made of plastic. "A flare gun," he said, showing her the cartridges that slipped inside the chamber.

"Will it hurt someone or do we just signal with it?"

"Damn right it'll hurt someone."

Thinking of their last attack and how close they'd come to being herded into a van and driven to who knows where, she said, "Good."

Repocketing the flares and the gun, he added, "I poured the leftover soup into a thermos and stowed it in the galley. Are you hungry?"

"Starved." She went down below and found the thermos. Wedging herself in a small nook, she drank the broth, gobbled the vegetables, chewed on a crusty chunk of bread. By the time she finished and had washed up after herself, the last of the nightmare had vanished and the black mood that had gripped her in its wake was gone. She took a deep breath of old boat tinged with salty air and climbed back out into the cockpit.

BLACK OUTLINES dotted the harbor, boats at anchor, massive shapes of power vessels, slimmer, sleeker shapes of sailboats. Running without lights and using the momentum of the hull, Will chose an out-of-the-way location and dropped the biggest anchor he could find.

Julia had been at the helm, taking direction. As soon as he pointed thumbs-up in her direction, she disappeared below deck.

Catching two halyards in his hands and leaning forward against the lifeline, Will peered ashore.

Twinkling lights pinpointed cliffside houses. He didn't know if anyone had seen him sail into the small cove—he doubted it and assumed that even if someone had, they wouldn't give it a second thought.

Down below he found Julia adding a bottle of water to her shoulder bag.

"Better take our passports," he said, and digging into the cigar box, added some of his aunt's emergency fund. The Euros were all but gone; they'd have to chance a bank. It would be stupid not to have local currency for their escape from the island once they rescued Leo. What he needed now was a discreet place to carry the flare gun.

"I have the passports," she said.

Will slid his bulky cotton sweater over his

head and pushed the empty flare gun inside the bandage wrapping his chest. He pulled the sweater back on without groaning out loud—no small feat. The cartridges went into his pocket.

Julia extinguished the lantern and they climbed the ladder and emerged into the cockpit.

Will untied the dinghy, bypassing the small motor in favor of quieter oars. He threw in a couple of life jackets while Julia deposited her bag. With the help of the winch, he lowered the dinghy into the water as Julia tied the painter to a stanchion. Holding Julia's hands, he lowered her into the dinghy, ignoring the sharp stabbing pain in his side, then followed himself, untying the painter before sitting. They pushed the smaller craft away from the big sailboat. Will took off shoes and socks and rolled his jeans in preparation for landing, then manned the oars.

Neither one of them spoke a word as Will rowed toward shore. The tide was coming in, making the job a little easier though the cracked rib cancelled that advantage. Julia whispered an offer of help, but he wanted to remain in control.

He'd anchored the *Marie Antoinette* so far out that it took a half hour before they felt the oars dig into the bottom of the bay. They rode the gentle surf toward the shore, oars out of the water. Will stowed the oars and jumped out of the dinghy, pulling its bow onto the sandy beach before helping Julia out. Together, they dragged the dingy higher up on the beach, away from the incoming tide, overturning it near a line of vegetation and rocks. The whitish gleam of boats stowed in similar fashion surrounded them. If their luck held, their dinghy would look like all the others when the sun rose. He sat atop the bottom of the dinghy and put his shoes back on, unrolling his jeans and shaking the sand off his hands.

"The road is right up there," Will said close to Julia's ear. "It's two and a quarter miles to Port Jewel."

"Let's go," she said, walking ahead of him, climbing a small incline and scrambling over a low rock fence. Keeping to the verge beside the road, they walked single file, Julia in front with the bag tossed over her shoulder, Will in the back, one hand gripping his side, the other gripping the flashlight though he tried not to use it.

The road was not well traveled this late at night. When they did hear a motor, they climbed back over the fence and ducked behind the rocks. It was uphill at first, then leveled off as it wound its way around the headland until the capital city of Port Jewel came into sight, nestled between mountains, glittering with a hundred thousand lights.

"It's beautiful," Julia said as they paused at the top of the last hill before heading into town. They'd both studied the guidebook by now and knew the castle sat on the southern bluff. The moon had risen and cast soft light over the opposing mountainside. The castle's pinkish walls glowed.

Will folded Julia's hand in his and pressed it against his chest, over his heart. He tried to define his feelings about the castle and the country he was seeing for the first time. This was his father's kingdom. Whatever these people were, he was, too. At least half of him was.

Thanks to a brief history and overview of the present political situation outlined in the guidebook, Will knew Montivitz had been invaded and occupied by many nations over the years and was a young monarchy, established late in the middle of the last century with a direct line of descendants through the Lévesque family. Federico Lévesque should have been next.

What the guidebook didn't say, because it hadn't happened at the time of publication, was that with Prince Federico's death, the line of ascension had become muddled, and the growing unrest at housing an American air base in the world's present political climate had escalated. There was an urgent call to abandon the monarchy and establish free elections.

Will was all for that. As for violence as a means to an end—that was another matter.

"What do you think?" Julia whispered against his cheek.

He turned to face her, drinking in the moonlit sight of her face. In a few short days, she, along with Leo, had become his reality.

"I think it's high time we got Leo the hell out of here."

THEY ENTERED the city near sunrise to find quaint cobblestone streets, bygones of the Italian occupation centuries before. Red tile roofs. Old buildings, narrow roads, flowers spilling from every window box, views of the boat-filled harbor around every corner.

They stopped at a small bakery and bought hot coffee and rolls to ward off the chill and pass a little time until the banks opened.

In person, Will had to amend his first impression of Montivitz, gathered from the photos on the cover of the guidebook. Sure the place was picturesque in an Old World way, but it wasn't plastic like a theme park. There were many real-world touches that tickled the senses. The slight smell of rotting fruit, the fumes from too many automobiles, garish display windows, stray dogs, even the occasional beggar made Port Jewel a city that could and did exist outside a controlled environment.

And that's what his housing development had lacked. The one he'd been designing when the boat blew up. In an attempt to make things charming, he'd relied on re-creating the past instead of interpreting the present and anticipating the future. Looking around him, he knew how to fix it. For the first time since the ordeal began, he itched to get back to his career.

"Penny for your thoughts," Julia whispered.

"Do you think an architect and a pilot and a little boy who is soon to be reunited with them both can all find happiness together?"

"If none of them get killed in the next few hours, I don't know," she said. "Maybe."

"No maybe about it," he said, draping an arm over her shoulder and nuzzling her ear. He was rewarded with a soft sigh.

As soon as the banks opened, Julia exchanged American dollars for Euros in preparation for any eventuality. Will wasn't crazy about her being the one to show her passport, but it was less likely her name would be recognized than his own. It came as a huge relief when she returned in one piece.

Attempting to look touristy, they ambled along the sidewalks. It was a little tricky as the average tourist wasn't dressed head to toe in black, but a quick purchase of a dark red sun hat for her and sunglasses for them both softened their look.

"You look too much like your father did when he was your age," Julia told him in an aside. "I've seen people looking at you. Wear the glasses."

For a beautiful April morning in a Mediterranean country, there was an air of tension in the city. The frequent sight of armed policemen might have accounted for some of it, but it seemed to go deeper. The people here spoke both Italian and French dialects, so Will could understand a smattering of the conversations going on around him. The unease was palpable, everyone seemed on edge, even the tourists appeared to be glancing over their shoulders. Small posters tacked up in obscure places urged people to get rid of the Americans. One man's face showed up again and again, fist raised above his head, unruly black hair framing a fierce face slashed with a black mustache, the words Take Back Montivitz emblazoned across his chest.

Paul Bernard. Poletier had mentioned this man in their phone conversation. Will's attempt to decipher the small print stopped when a policeman grunted with displeasure and tore the poster from the wall.

They found a tram that, for a token price, carted tourists up and down the palace hill every hour on the hour. They purchased two tickets. The ride took only a few minutes and they disembarked with everyone else in a circular area outside the open palace gates, providing a tantalizing view of a huge court-yard. Armed guards wearing blue tunics stood on either side of the gate. A few rock buildings surrounding the palace were accessed by a winding cobbled path shaded by large flowering bushes and deep eaves. Will looked from the path to the guards. He met stony, intense stares.

"Let's find another way," he said.

Hand in hand, they wandered off on their own, casing the place, wondering what to do next. They found a circle of stone benches near the bluff and took a seat on an empty one.

"We should have brought a camera," Julia said, nodding toward a group of tourists snapping multiple pictures of the castle. It was easy to see why they did.

The palace itself was much older than the Lévesque rule, built in the late sixteenth century by the Italians. It had all the proper castle-like accoutrements. Towering over one hundred and fifty feet above them, twin spires framed the gates while battlements scalloped the top. In times long gone, soldiers would have patrolled, protecting the castle from the next invading army.

"I say we march up to the guards and demand to see the king," Will said. "You say I look like my father. Maybe someone will notice the resemblance and let me inside."

"Minister Poletier said it would be dangerous for you to show up on Montivitz right now," Julia protested. "Besides, are you forgetting about that letter? One look at you and we might get a one-way ticket to ye old dungeon. This is your idea of finesse?"

"But—"

A soft honking caught their attention. Will looked up to see a long open car with flags flapping on either side of the windshield. Several stony-faced men wearing beribboned uniforms rode in the car, which drove through the castle gates.

"There must be a meeting," Julia said.

Will narrowed his eyes. "Maybe I'll crash it."

As they stared at each other trying to figure out if that would work, a loud explosion shattered the stillness of the valley below. Both he and Julia jumped to their feet and ran toward the bluff, peering down the hillside toward Port Jewel where a plume of black smoke spiraled upward. Within seconds, sirens blared from all directions, converging on the scene of the explosion. Up on the bluff, other people gathered, pointing and talking.

"What was that?" Julia whispered.

"I don't know," Will said, but what he was

thinking was that maybe it was providence knocking at their door.

Another blast in a different part of the city erupted just then, adding to the general air of turmoil. Will glanced back at the guards. Some had rushed to join the knot of people staring down into the city and others had turned to talk to someone in the courtyard.

Providence, all right.

Will took Julia's hand and led her to the heavy shadows cast by a trio of trees. Glancing over his shoulder, he found the guards still reacting to the confusion. Hand in hand, he and Julia skirted the clearing, making for the smaller buildings adjoining the palace, looking for an unguarded back door.

No shouts. No whistles, no gunfire. A third explosion, sounding farther away this time, covered their footsteps as they rushed down the path. What was happening down in the city? The timing was advantageous, but the explosions themselves sounded ominous. Was this the beginning of the forecasted riots?

The path ended at a door that had to be centuries old. Eight feet high and half as wide, it was made of nine-inch thick planks held together with bands of metal riveted into the wood. The wall in which it was set consisted of the same pinkish stone that comprised the rest of the castle. It towered forty or fifty feet above their heads. There was no outside lock, no way through, no way over or around.

"Dead end," Julia murmured.

They hurried back down the path, pausing this time to check the doors of the buildings, finding each one locked. Peering through a window, Will saw empty offices. Looked as though the palace business was in a slump.

The disturbance beyond the path had quieted down, the crowd gathered at the bluff now dispersing. At least three fires could be seen issuing smoke down in the city. Will and Julia reclaimed their bench, Will's mind racing, trying to come up with a new plan.

Julia scooted closer to him as someone sat down on her other side. She issued a soft greeting.

"Miss Sheridan," the newcomer said.

With the mention of her name, Julia's whole body tensed. Will looked over her head and met the limpid brown gaze of a man nearing seventy.

"I did not expect you to come to the castle," the man said, directing his comment to Will.

"Minister Poletier. How did you know—"

"That you were on Montivitz?" The old man paused, appearing to weigh his words. "The bank alerted me."

"But how did they recognize my name?" Julia said.

"It was known Mr. Wellspring traveled as William Noble and that he purchased your ticket at the same time, Miss Sheridan. This was not difficult to ascertain."

"Did you send an oversized thug to Toulon to intercept us?" Will asked, point-blank.

Poletier studied Julia's cut and bruised cheek before he answered. "Certainly not."

"Then who do you suppose sent him?"

"He must have been one of Paul Bernard's men," Poletier said, disgust lifting one lip. "They are all brutes."

"How would Bernard know anything about me?"

"He has spies within the palace. He may even be tapping phones," Poletier replied, adding, "Did you bring a gun into Monti-

vitz? Our laws concerning imported fire-
arms are quite…inflexible."

"No," Will said.

Poletier directed his gaze outward and
raised a hand in the general direction of the
bluff. White hair still thick, he wore a
charcoal suit and a white shirt so well tailored
they screamed *designer.* A tie clip, enameled
with a crest, secured a red tie. Three rings,
each studded with gems, dominated gnarled
hands.

"The riots have started," Poletier said, his
voice raspy. "Paul Bernard and his followers
are determined to overthrow the monarchy."

"Why doesn't the king stop him?"

Poletier gazed out at the city for an interminable time before replying. "Bernard is
wily. He and others like him drum up
support from differing factions. For a small
island, Montivitz offers many places to hide
and the coasts of several other countries are
nearby. You, Mr. Wellspring, are in great
danger. You have put Miss Sheridan in
danger. I asked you not to come. I told you
I would take care of…things."

"Yes. But I told you then my concern is
not for your country. It's for my son. Julia
shares that concern."

Poletier's gaze drifted back to Will's face. "I hadn't realized you'd grown to look so much like your father," he said. "And like your brother, Federico."

"Minister Poletier," Julia said, touching the old man's sleeve. "What about Leo?"

"He is safe. I have talked to the adoptive family."

"His kidnappers, you mean," Will said, fury burning his throat. "You alerted them?"

"I mean to find a peaceful solution," Poletier said. "They are reasonable people."

"They are kidnappers and murderers," Will said, eyes blazing. Julia put a hand on his sleeve. He took a deep breath. "These people have taken my son, Poletier. It's cut and dry."

"On the contrary," Poletier said, his voice halting. "I have discovered they were given the child by another...official."

"Who?"

"They refuse to divulge this person's identity. They were told the child was related to the king and that as an orphan with no one to protect him, his life would be in jeopardy considering the current...situation...on Montivitz. They took him as a great kindness, you see."

"Why won't they tell who gave them my son?"

"Perhaps they were threatened. I assure you, there will be a thorough investigation."

"You do understand the devastation to lives and property that has come about in this reckless pursuit of Leo, don't you?" Julia said.

"It's my father, isn't it?" Will said. Don't bother defending him, Poletier. I know about the letter you sent my aunt, the one giving an unnamed henchman carte blanche to do away with my aunt and myself."

Poletier shook his head. "I had hoped your aunt might have destroyed that...communication. She wouldn't take me seriously. I had to convince her. But that was long ago."

"To me it was yesterday."

Into the following uneasy silence, Julia said, "There's a meeting of some kind going on in the castle."

"The police are here. Demonstrators threaten more bombings. Already the streets are full of young people turning over cars and starting fires."

"What about the American government? Aren't they taking part in this? It's their—it's our—military base."

"The king has requested they not interfere."

Will took a deep breath. "I *will* get inside the castle and take back my son. If you won't help me, at least don't try to stop me."

Poletier's head bobbed. Hard to tell if it was a yes, no or maybe. He said, "The adoptive parents are willing to meet with you and talk."

"Talk!"

"Maybe we should take what we can get," Julia said.

Will stared hard at Poletier, trying to read the older man, having no luck. "Okay, let's go. Right now."

"Most unadvisable, sir. We cannot parade you inside the castle. If your father saw you—"

"Then sneak me in."

"Tonight," Poletier said. "There is a house at the bottom of the hill. It will be safe for you to stay there for the rest of the day. Paul Bernard must not catch wind of your presence on the island. After dark—"

"At least Paul Bernard sounds like a man of action," Will said.

Poletier all but shuddered. "Watch what you say, sir. I need a few hours. I must speak with the family. These things take time. Be patient."

"Stop calling them Leo's *family,*" Will snapped. Poletier bowed his head as he turned away.

Chapter Ten

Poletier arranged to have them driven to a small house at the base of the hill, their driver a deferential man as old as Poletier. He spent the short trip talking about Montivitz. Though he spoke English, his accent was so thick Julia couldn't understand much of what he said.

The house they arrived at consisted of two stories of whitewashed walls and the ubiquitous pots of spring flowers. The driver insisted on opening car doors. He then bowed his farewell and drove away as a beefy man with a shaved head came out of the house. Without speaking, the new man gestured at the front door and plopped himself down on a bench. As Will held the door open for Julia, she glanced back. The bald man caught her glance. His expression didn't change.

Inside, they found a diminutive woman with a tidy graying bun and close-set black eyes. She showed them to a table and began laying out plates and bowls of food. The scent of flowers drifted though a pair of open windows set into the stone.

The little woman relieved Julia of her bags, smiled a lot and nodded, but she didn't speak to them. Julia and Will both picked at plates of fruit and cheese, ignoring the carafe of wine, choosing bottled water instead.

After lunch, the little woman bustled them out into an enclosed courtyard where Julia supposed they were to cool their heels until Poletier came for them. The top story of the house extended beyond the bottom story by about three feet, creating an overhang that protected the dining room doors and windows from sun and rain. Beyond the overhang, the Mediterranean sun filtered through the leaves of olive trees.

"I don't like this," Will said, pacing back and forth, one hand clutching his side. The courtyard was long and narrow but cluttered with a round table, two wooden chairs and numerous flowerpots, making the pacing more like dodging. He stopped and stared down at Julia who had collapsed onto one of the chairs. "Poletier is calling all the shots."

"He didn't search you. You still have the flare gun."

"You want me to blast that nice little woman?"

"No. Of course not."

Sitting down in the other chair, he added, "That damn Poletier is treating this like a diplomatic problem and not a kidnapping."

Julia got up from her wooden chair and dragged it across the patio and through the flower garden. Jamming it up against the rock wall, she climbed up on the seat, then onto the broad arm. What she saw when she peeked over the top did nothing to comfort her and she climbed down.

Will had turned to study the back of the house.

Julia dragged the chair back to its rightful place. Will talked to her from over his shoulder. "Did you see anything?" he asked.

"Just the bald guy. He has a shotgun. I wonder if Poletier knows we're being guarded?"

"Of course he knows."

"To keep us in or Paul Bernard and his buddies out?"

"Maybe a little of both."

"What are you staring at?" she asked Will.

"The house."

"As an architect?"

"Kind of. Did you understand what the old guy who drove us down the hill was talking about?"

"No. His English was dreadful."

"He talked about this house. Said it was built at the same time as the castle. The king owns it now."

"So?"

"The back is odd. Look at the windows."

Except for one place on the bottom floor, sets of two windows broke up the pinkish rock surface. In this single space, there was just one window instead of two. It was located close to the overhang and Julia could tell it was this that had caught Will's attention. "Maybe it's a bathroom," she said.

"Buildings this old don't have bathrooms."

"But if someone renovated—"

"Why take out the window? And even if they did, the stone would look different when they filled in the wall. That wall is original material."

"What are you saying?"

Will's answer was cut short by the arrival of the housekeeper who delivered a tray of lemonade and two glasses.

Ignoring the beverage, Will folded his hands together and rested his cheek on them as if sleeping. He pointed at Julia and at himself and again, mimed sleep.

The woman nodded. Waving them inside, she led them down the hall, pausing in front of an open door. A glance inside revealed a narrow room with two twin beds and an open window looking out on the courtyard they'd just exited.

Will took a quick spin of the room. He shook his head and moved on down the hall, the little woman trailing after him.

He stopped at the end of the hall, peering through a door on his right. Looking over the housekeeper's head, he called, "Come on, Julia. This is the room we want."

What was he doing? She stood there perplexed as he marched back down the hall and scooped her into his arms. His face reflected the agony this gesture must have had on his cracked rib. She said, "Are you crazy?"

"No doubt," he said, the grimace transforming into a big grin as he turned around and carried her back down the hall, past the housekeeper, into the room. He tossed her onto a big fluffy white bed.

Julia stared up at him, speechless.

Dropping his fists onto the pillow on either side of her head, he leaned down and proceeded to kiss her in that hungry, hot way he had so that by the time he drew back, she was ready to strip off her clothes and drag him between the sheets. She had a feeling she looked as dazed as she felt.

He got up and walked to the door, propelled the housekeeper out of the room and closed the door behind her. The housekeeper's giggles followed her retreat up the hall.

"What are you up to?" Julia whispered as Will returned to the bed. It was crazy, but that one kiss had primed her for more.

"The first room we were shown is the one with a single window," he said.

"You and your windows," she muttered as she got to her feet, straightened her sweater and ran a hand through her hair. It had come loose and she gathered it into a ponytail again, searching the floor for her new red hat which had come off somewhere along the way. "Okay, what's up?"

"Look around you."

She registered a bed pushed against the interior wall, skirted by tables and lamps on either side. A carved wardrobe occupied the wall opposite the door. The two big open windows emptied right back into the enclosed courtyard. What had they gained by coming inside the house? She looked back at him and raised her eyebrows.

"There's no linen closet," he said.

"What?"

"In the hall. Just blank space."

"Huh?"

"There are two bedrooms downstairs on this side of the house. We've seen them both. Both have an interior wooden wall. But there's about three and a half feet missing between the rooms and it's not closets because both rooms have their beds pushed up tight against the wood and there was no opening off the hall."

"And all this means?"

He smiled patiently. "It's a very old structure. It's right below the castle. It's missing three and a half feet of ground-level interior space. It's owned by the king."

She stared into his eyes until comprehension caused her jaw to drop. "Are you saying there's a secret way up to the castle right here in this room?"

"If we're lucky it's in this room. If it's not, we'll have to have a loud fight and demand separate beds so we can search the other room. I have a feeling it's in here."

Even as he spoke, he ran his hands over the wood behind the bed. It took him almost five minutes of checking the ceiling, the floor and every square inch in between before he issued a low whistle, pulled the bed out from the wall, moved the left table and lamp, and pushed against the floorboard with his foot.

A click announced success as the wall seemed to crack open on an invisible vertical seam.

"Beautiful workmanship," Will said, running a hand down the wood. Julia joined him and they both peered into the dark interior behind the secret panel.

The pull of a dangling cord ignited a single overhead bulb, revealing a trapdoor on the floor. The trapdoor opened without a squeak. A dark staircase led into oblivion.

"The housekeeper never gave me back my bag," Julia said. "I don't have a flashlight."

"Or our passports," Will said. He peered

down into the hole. "We have to take this chance," he said after a moment. "We can't sit here and depend on Poletier. He's too timid. I made a mistake letting him trap us in this house and now that we have a chance to escape—"

"We have to take it," Julia said. "I agree." Inside, she quaked. Loose in a foreign country without a passport? And how could they find their way in the darkness beyond with no light?

As Will locked the bedroom door, Julia searched the wardrobe, hoping to find a light source. She came up with two blankets, an empty hot water bottle and an extra pillow. When she turned back to the room, she found Will had shuttered the windows and pushed the furniture back into place. Except for the narrow opening in the wall, the room looked much as it had before. They sidled their way into the opening, then Will repositioned the lamp table.

"Look," Julia said, relief making her legs weak. She'd found a kerosene lamp hanging in back of the trapdoor. The matchbox under it held dry matches.

"Things are looking up."

"Won't they figure out where we've

gone?" Julia said as Will lit the kerosene lantern. It cast a yellow glow into the chamber and illuminated the first few steps leading down.

"I doubt the housekeeper or the guard outside know about this passage," Will said as he closed the hidden door. "No doubt Poletier knows so we need to hurry. Still, I think our little act gave us a couple of hours of uninterrupted privacy. It's still midafternoon."

"That was an act?" Julia said, fanning her face.

He kissed her, his eyes twinkling in the flickering light. "No, that was a wish and a promise."

Holding the lantern, Will insisted on descending first. He caught Julia's hand as she stepped off the last stair and onto a packed-dirt floor.

The lantern illuminated a small cave-like area, a tunnel leading upward from one end. Webs hung in the dank, still air. Julia peered ahead into the gloom. As she took the first tentative steps, she recalled the tram ride up the mountain. If this tunnel led to the castle, they had a long trek ahead of them. She picked up her pace, listening for the sounds of pursuit, dodging webs and debris, wishing she were almost anywhere else on earth.

WILL'S SIDE was killing him. He should never have picked up Julia, though he hadn't been able to come up with a faster way to show their housekeeper what he had in mind.

The tunnel wasn't quite tall enough for him and he had to bend forward a bit as he walked. There were places his shoulders brushed the sides of the tunnel, other places where the sides had caved in and they had to scramble through the loose dirt.

He knew each step forward was a step in elevation, but after the first few hundred feet, the passage twisted so much he couldn't place where they were in relation to the castle. There was nothing to do but move along as fast as they could.

Ahead of him, Julia's breathing grew more labored. His conscience got the better of him for a moment and he lagged, considering the impact he'd had on her life in the past few days. Though she'd insisted on being a part of this, the truth was he'd wanted her with him; he hadn't fought hard enough to leave her behind. Even now, he couldn't find it in his heart to regret her involvement.

He had to deliver her home. He had to find Leo. He would protect them both with his life but would it be enough?

It took an hour before the tunnel evened out and the walking got easier. The headroom also improved and Will was able to straighten up at last and roll his shoulders. It ended when they turned a corner and were confronted with a flight of earthen stairs, leading up.

"Wait a second," he said, brushing sticky cobwebs from his face and hair. He lifted his sweater and Julia helped free the flare gun. He loaded it, made sure the safety was on, and stuck it in his pocket for easy access.

"Okay," he said. "I'll go first. If something happens I can't solve with a direct hit from the flare gun, give yourself up, don't try to fight."

She nodded. He stared down at her face, at the swollen cheek and angry gash, at her deep brown eyes and perfect lips curved into a brave smile. He wiped a cobweb from her brow. Then he turned and climbed the stairs.

The light played over a plain old door with

an old-fashioned lock. A key hung from a big ring looped over a hook next to the door. Will unlocked the door, somewhat relieved when it seemed difficult to do so. Did that mean it wasn't used much, that people may have forgotten about it?

He replaced the key and pushed on the wooden panel, breath suspended. He waited for some sound of discovery. When none came, he opened it wider.

It led into a narrow curved passageway, two-stories high and best of all, empty. Light came in through windows twenty feet overhead so it was possible to see into the dimness. Will turned back to Julia and motioned for her to join him. "So far, so good," he whispered as he blew out the lantern and left it sitting by the door.

After the earthy stuffiness of the tunnel, the passage seemed fresh, almost breezy, and yet it wasn't a typical hallway. Too narrow, no doors leading off it. The walls were made of stone, the floors covered in a very old and very thick carpet, giving no impression of recent wear.

It was obvious to Will that they were in a rounded part of the castle, perhaps one of the turrets. When the passage ended at the foot of a steep flight of stone stairs, he led the way. They spiraled upward until they reached the top and were confronted once again with a curved corridor much like the one they'd just left. This one wasn't as lofty and was somewhat darker.

Will had just descended a flight of stairs ahead of them when he became aware of a male voice coming from somewhere nearby. Stopping dead in his tracks, he turned to face Julia.

She pointed at a small grate by her shoulder. She touched the grating and it fell away without a sound, revealing a hole through which light shone. The voice became louder.

Will could see Julia's profile as she bent to peer through the opening. Stepping aside, she made a gesture for him to take a peek.

A piece of cloth, gauze or something just as diaphanous, blurred the details in the room beyond, all viewed from the vantage point of behind and above an aqua-covered bed. Will caught a glimpse of paneled walls, baroque furniture and a door on the opposite wall.

A man spoke to someone out of sight. As tall as Will but much thinner, he was dressed in light-colored slacks and shirt, his fair hair, making him appear almost wraithlike. His features were distorted by the gauze, but his body language, as he tore off his necktie and threw it on the floor, screamed anger. He spoke the Montivitz dialect Will had trouble understanding, though one word delivered with a stabbing motion in thin air stopped Will's heart for a count of five. *Tuer.*

Kill.

A woman's voice answered, high-pitched, bordering on hysteria. She spoke the same dialect but with a different accent, and remained outside Will's limited field of vision.

As Will pondered the wisdom of sticking around to see if he could decipher what they were arguing about, another sound sent his pulse into overdrive.

A baby's cries, coming from somewhere deep in the room.

Will straightened up so fast he collided with Julia who had tilted her head next to his. They made a grab for each other, steadying themselves, her hands clasping his arms, his gripping hers. Their eyes met in the light from the opening. She mouthed, "Leo?"

He nodded, every cell in his body galvanized. From behind the panel, the argument raged on, Leo's cries unattended. In single file, Will and Julia continued down the passage, ignoring additional panels, searching for a way out.

JULIA'S HEART leapt as they neared the end of the passage. Once again, it morphed into a flight of stairs, but this time, instead of climbing, they felt around for an exit. Julia felt a knob and clutched Will's arm. He turned to her, touching his lips with a single finger. He needn't worry. Her mouth was so dry she doubted she could utter a squeak let alone a word.

As Will's hand closed over the knob, they heard a door slam close by. And then came a crash.

They emerged from behind a screen into a small room lit by several lamps, papered in flocked red, cluttered with ornate furniture.

Will pulled Julia into his arms and lowered his lips to her ear. A sense of security defied their present circumstances. His embrace could do that, even in the lion's den.

"Did you hear a crash?"

She licked dry lips. "Someone threw something."

"I don't hear Leo anymore. Judging from the passage we just left, I'd say we've been in a kind of secret hallway with spy holes looking into other rooms. Unless they took him away, Leo's got to be on this side of the castle, very close judging from the short distance we traveled. We have to get to him."

"I counted two more of those hidden panels as we passed," Julia said.

"Sounds like we want the room two doors down."

In unison, they turned to the next door in their way, this one made of rich dark wood with a band of light at the bottom. It opened into a wide, well-lit hallway hung with portraits, painted a warm gold, paneled with gleaming wood. It, too, was empty.

How long could their luck hold? A place like this had to be crawling with guards.

They walked as fast as they could without making noise but the hall wasn't carpeted and the squeak of their shoes grated against taut nerves. At the third door along, they came to a stop and listened again. A baby's cry floated like music on the wind. Julia felt a knot form in her throat.

Footsteps echoing along the hall behind them propelled them to take their chances inside the room. They stepped over a shattered vase and the white roses the vase had once held before being smashed against the door. The baby's cries became sharper. Julia's gaze flew to the opposite wall where she found a huge bed, covered with aqua brocade, backed with sheer drapes. They'd looked through those drapes to see the man who had been in this room until moments before.

Will picked up an abandoned necktie from the floor, then nodded toward a narrow door to the side through which they could hear a woman crooning assurances. As the door stood ajar, they moved to avoid the woman's peripheral vision, their footfalls cushioned in thick cashmere carpets and masked by the baby's sobs.

The adjacent room was a nursery and as far away from the modest attempts Julia had made to make a home for Leo as night is from day. Done in a dozen shades of blue and gold, it looked like a miniature palace itself, every stuffed animal known to mankind in attendance, every possible need anticipated and provided for.

A nursery for a prince.

But as grand as the nursery appeared, what took center stage were the two figures near the crib. A woman stood with her back to them, thick dark hair streaming past her shoulders, clothed in a sleeveless white dress, long legs bare, a baby cradled in her arms. The top of the child's head was all they could see. Reddish hair, fine and silky. Hair like Leo's.

The child's sobs segued into hiccups. Julia's jaw clenched, her fingers twitched at her side. She looked up at Will and found the expression in his eyes downright explosive. Wrapping either end of the necktie in his hands, he stretched it tight, ready to encircle the woman's neck. Thank heavens he wasn't aiming to shoot her with the flare gun.

At that moment, she must have sensed their presence, for she twirled to face them, clutching the baby to her chest, his face buried against her shoulder, one of her hands covering the back of his neck.

She sucked in air when she saw them. Julia's mouth dropped open. The woman and she looked enough alike to be sisters. Same build, same coloring, same age. In fact, Julia had seen this woman once before, in the San Francisco airport, carrying a baby, accompanied by a tall man.

The man she'd seen through the grill. The fake George Abbot.

The woman's eyes were red and moist, her face tearstained, flushed. She looked from Julia to Will and her eyes narrowed as though trying to place him.

She spoke words unintelligible to Julia. Will said, "Do you speak English?"

"Of course," she responded, her accent thick. "How did you get in here?" How could Pepin have ever taken this woman for an American?

"I came for my son," Will said, ignoring her question. "Give him to me."

"Then it's true." Her eyes grew wide again. "You are the king's son! You are poor Federico's older brother. I thought you were dead." As she spoke, her accent became more and more American.

This time Will's eyes narrowed. "You're the one who called me that night, aren't you? I recognize your voice. You set me up."

"I am good with voices," she said, bravado easing some of the distress on her face. "I spent three years studying in California colleges."

"And you impersonated me at the airport," Julia added. "Who *are* you?"

"You may call me Renee. Who I am is of no matter."

Will strode across the room and took the baby from Renee's arms. Her empty hands floated down to her sides, her eyes looked stricken.

Will peered down at the baby and the smile and relief that flooded his eyes told Julia all she needed to know. They'd found Leo.

Leo, hiccups still coming, kicked his blankets free. A geyser of pure relief spouted in Julia's heart at the sight of his chubby pink toes. He was safe, he was alive, he was theirs again.

She hadn't failed him after all.

The baby grabbed Will's nose and smiled a toothless grin, head bobbing with the effort. Disengaging his son's tiny hands, Will kissed Leo's forehead and hugged him tightly before placing him in Julia's outstretched hands.

"Hello, baby Leo," Julia crooned, and held him so tightly against herself that he squealed. She didn't need to see the strawberry mark to know this was Nicole's baby and she hugged him for her late cousin as well. Whatever faults Nicole had had, she'd loved her baby, she'd deserved the chance to watch him grow up. Julia buried her face against Leo's neck, drinking in his sweet baby scent.

"Yes, I impersonated you, Miss Sheridan," Renee said. "I was told you did not want this baby. Albert impersonated your fiancé."

"But George Abbot wasn't my fiancé."

"The material we had on you was... outdated."

"And me?" Will snapped. "You called my office and—"

"Pretended to be a policeman's wife, yes. But I thought you were only to be distracted. And I didn't know they would kill your wife. Or your aunt. Please, you have to leave. Go before Albert returns. Your baby is no longer safe here."

"Who's Albert?" Julia demanded.

"My husband. Please, he said when he returned he would kill the baby. He said the child is a liability. Take him. Go back the way you came."

"What about Minister Poletier? Didn't he talk to you about us coming to reclaim my son?"

"I have not seen him today. Please, do as I ask. Go back the way you came."

"We can't," Will said. He took a few steps, motioning for Julia to join him. Lowering his voice to a whisper, he cradled his son's soft thigh as he leaned in close to her ear. "Looks like Albert is behind things. Maybe in cahoots with my father, maybe one of Paul Bernard's men, planted in the castle to destroy from within. Poletier must have told Albert we'd come for Leo and now Albert's getting ready to cut his losses. We're going to have to exit this castle by a different route. If we can make it back to the *Marie Antoinette,* we can be out to sea before anyone knows to look for us."

"If the wind blows," Julia said.

"True." He regarded Renee for a moment before saying, "Show us how to get out of here."

The panic reflected on her face skyrocketed. "No."

"You must help us," Julia pleaded. "Leo is in danger. Leave with us if you're afraid for yourself. Just help us save this baby. Show us how to get out of here without being seen."

Renee twisted her hands together, bit her lip.

"Renee, please," Julia said as she grabbed a diaper bag she spied by the changing table. Leo chose that moment to reach out to Renee whose eyes filled with new tears as she moved closer.

She folded his tiny fist in her hand and kissed it. "I will do this for him," she announced. "For the little one." And with that decision came action. She produced a couple of bottles of milk from a concealed refrigerator, handing them to Julia who stowed them in the diaper bag. "Don't speak to anyone," she cautioned, exiting the nursery and grabbing a sweater from the back of a chair. "Quick. There isn't much time. If we're caught…"

She didn't finish the sentence. There was no need to finish it.

Chapter Eleven

Holding his son in his arms, Will followed Renee down the broad hallway, Julia right behind him.

His son. Safe. His small warm body clutched against Will's heart. A miracle. Now all they had to do was escape.

Renee led them up a short flight of stairs and along yet another corridor. They passed several groups of uniformed people who spared them little more than a curious glance. It was obvious Renee was a well-known figure in the castle and enjoyed certain privileges.

Somewhere in this edifice of stone-and-gold mortared together with secrets, resided his father, no doubt meeting with dignitaries or police, perhaps alerted by Poletier that his son was in Montivitz. Maybe the outside riots were keeping him busy. Maybe Paul Bernard was more of a worry than a renegade son.

Will fought the desire to confront his father, a desire that grew more urgent with each step. How would they reenter America without their passports? How in the world would he and Julia and Leo ever be safe if they didn't put an end to this right now? Was he destined to spend his adult years as he had his childhood, using false identities, running and hiding? He could not raise Leo that way. He wouldn't. And how about Julia? What would living in the shadows do to her life?

He stopped walking. Renee turned to him. "What is it?"

He shook his head and resumed walking, but the conviction grew that leaving here without settling things was a stop-gap measure at best. The one person who could make sure he and his were left alone to lead their lives was the one person who had wanted him dead since the day he was born—his father.

Ahead of them, a man backed out of a room holding a tray upon which sat a half-empty goblet of something red. He was followed by another man. This one impressive in a royal-blue tunic, carrying a staff. The servant closed the door, glanced over his shoulder at Renee, bowed his head and hurried off. The guard with the staff took his place beside the door.

If this wasn't destiny, what was?

He said, "That's my father's suite, isn't it?"

"Yes," Renee said. "Hurry."

"No. I need to see him."

"No," Renee said.

Glancing back at Julia, Will held out a hand and she took it. Renee made feeble sounds of protest.

"Are you sure you want to do this?" Julia asked as they crossed the hall.

"It's the only way. Without him backing down, we'll never be free. Maybe it'll be harder to order our deaths if he sees us face-to-face. You understand, don't you?"

She studied his eyes. "I guess I always knew it would come to this. Let's get it over with."

Will faced the guard, baby in his arms, Julia by his side. Speaking French, he said, "I'm entering this room."

The guard glanced at Renee who waved an irritated hand and rattled off directions.

The guard stood aside.

The area they entered was as big as a mansion with just about as many rooms. Doorways opened on both sides of a central corridor revealing opulent sitting rooms, meeting rooms, bedrooms, pantries. The gleam from gold and crystal, the burnished glow of fine wood, the thick carpets of muted colors and fabric-covered walls merged together to create an extravagant world unlike any Will had ever seen. He glanced at Julia, wondering what she thought of all this wealth. Her whole house would have fitted in the dining room.

His step faltered for a moment. All this was his birthright. All this could be his. And Leo's. Why should he walk away? How many men had the opportunity to be a king, to live in such splendor, to make a difference in a small piece of the world? So what if his father wanted him dead? He had Leo back. Just why should he leave Montivitz? Maybe he'd been going about this all wrong.

Julia squeezed his hand. When their eyes met, she smiled. He swore she could read his mind.

Renee caught up with them. "I don't see

why you want to see your—the king. What's the point?"

As they approached closed double doors with additional guards posted on either side, Will said, "He's in there?"

"He spends most of his time here. But—"

"Is he alone?" Will asked the guard. He didn't want to march into a room full of high-placed officials or police.

Renee translated Will's query. The guard nodded.

"I guess you have the right to see him," Renee said. "But be careful, make it brief."

"I'm seeing him to assure the continued safety of my family," Will replied, encircling Julia's shoulders to include her in this definition.

"I'm not sure what you expect of the king," Renee protested. "You must know—"

"That he's behind all this?" Will snapped. "Yeah, I know."

The guard said something else to Renee and she nodded. He opened the door and stood back as they stepped inside.

Will had expected to see an older version of himself sitting on a throne, passing an idle hour by counting gold coins or surrounded by important men, issuing edicts.

He hadn't expected a glorified bedroom. He hadn't expected drawn drapes, a muted television set flickering images into the gloom. Tables covered with bottles and potions. The smell of age, of illness.

"He must be sick," Will said.

Julia muttered, "The article I read said he was grieving. It didn't say anything about illness."

As Leo gurgled in his ear, Will looked down at the man lying in the luxurious bed.

His father.

A stranger.

Will took the flare gun from his pocket and switched off the safety. He handed it to Julia. "Watch the door," he said, turning back to the figure in the bed.

The old man opened his eyes. Gray eyes, like Will's, wrinkled cheeks clean shaven, complexion translucent. Features drawn, giving him a haunted, desperate look.

The king said something Will couldn't understand, his voice stronger than Will would have suspected. Will answered him in English. If Theodore Lévesque had spent time in the United States, if he'd won the heart of a young American girl, he must know English. "I need to talk to you," Will said.

The king struggled into a sitting position, resting his curved back against the pillows before touching Leo's dangling foot. "Little Federico," he said. He waved a hand at Will and added, "Leave the prince with me. You may come back later."

Staring down at his father, Will said, "Federico is…gone. Get up if you can, hear me out. It's the least you can do after all the mayhem you've caused."

The old man closed his eyes. When he opened them again, he said, "Where's my crown?"

Will blinked a couple of times before saying, "I don't know where your crown is. Listen—"

"Federico will rule after me. When he is grown, when he is a man. He is a baby now. But he will grow, strong and able. Like me. Like my father before me."

"What about your oldest son, King Theodore? What about the son born in America? Shouldn't he be king?" This from Julia, who had abandoned her post by the door and was now standing at Will's elbow.

The king seemed to notice her for the first

time. He said, "*That* son died with his mother." With a surprising burst of energy, the old man threw back the bedcovers and sat up straighter, swinging his feet to the floor.

He sat there for a moment, dressed in white pajamas, the smooth, refined fabric at odds with his coarse, dry skin.

"Who are you?" he demanded, staring into Will's eyes.

"I'm William Wellspring, Michelle's son."

The king shook his head. "Never heard of her."

"You met her in the United States a long time ago."

The king's face contorted, brows furrowing, spittle collecting on his thin lips. "What have you done to Federico?" And with that, he popped to his feet, catching Will off guard. Will lunged to catch his father with his free arm, but the old man twisted away, collapsing to the floor beside the bed, emaciated body heaving with silent sobs.

Will turned, thrusting Leo toward Julia who dropped the flare gun on the bed to take the baby. Will dropped to his knees beside his father. Any remaining hope of meaningful dialogue about past, present or future was squashed under the harsh glare of this reality. There would be no help from his father, nor had his father the wherewithal to orchestrate the events of the past few weeks. The old king was a dead end.

The king reached back, swatting at Will's attempts to help. How long had Theodore Lévesque been spiraling into dementia? Had the death of Federico accelerated the process?

The outer door burst open. Poletier marched in, accompanied by a half-dozen armed guards. Will was happy to see him. He might be older than his father, he might be slow and methodical and way too cautious, but at least his brain still worked.

"Minister Poletier," Will said, standing. "I—"

"He's trying to kill the king!" Poletier announced. "He's working with Paul Bernard. So is the woman. Search them."

"Julia, get the flare gun!" Will yelled.

She made a valiant dive for the flare gun but was stopped by two men who pulled her back. Will cursed them both and moved to knock them away from his woman and his child.

He didn't get far. Two more guards caught his arms.

"Take them to the portrait room, keep them under guard. Yes, the child, too," Poletier directed. "Call the king's doctors. Now!"

All of this was said in French, Will assumed, for his benefit. The guards understood for they circled the three of them, guns drawn. They looked angry and excited, a scary combination.

"What's going on?" Julia asked.

Will's gaze met Poletier's. Gone was the watery gaze of an aging man, in its place a fiery determination that took twenty years off his age. Poletier's lips twisted into a smile. In English, Poletier said, "You've outlived your usefulness, William Wellspring. You and your son."

"Clearing the throne for yourself."

He bowed his head. "I have been as good as a king for twenty years. But my son, Albert, will be a true king."

"It's been you all along, hasn't it?" Will said. "My father never knew I existed. You told him I died with my mother during childbirth."

"He didn't want to know," Poletier said.

"He left everything to me. And now he's past caring."

"And it was you who killed Nicole and Fiona. You who stole Leo—"

"I cannot take all the credit." He motioned the guards who moved still closer. "Take them," he said.

Will lifted Leo into his arms as Julia slipped her hand into his. Without a weapon, there wasn't a thing he could do but allow them to be led from the room. Julia's hand trembled in his.

Renee was nowhere in sight.

"Maybe this is the way Poletier plans on getting us out of the castle," Julia said, stroking Leo's bare leg as they walked. "Maybe he's just making a show of it. Maybe this is his way of saving us."

Will didn't have the heart to tell her she was dead wrong.

MOST OF the guards stayed outside the door of the portrait room, but two followed them inside, posting themselves by the only exit.

Will and Julia stared at each other in silence until Leo started fussing. Julia took the baby, and settling herself in a chair, produced a bottle of milk from the diaper bag. "At least it's not a dungeon," she said, gazing around the well-appointed room.

Leo ate with gusto, his hands rolled into fists with the effort. Julia, holding his son, made a beautiful bittersweet sight.

Leo fell asleep as he finished his bottle. Julia rose, burping the baby, then settled him on the silk brocade cushion of a dainty settee. As she wandered off to look at a row of royal portraits, Will covered his son with a blanket and stepped back. A string of milky drool, poised to roll off Leo's chin onto the pricey cushion, came close to eliciting a smile from his lips.

The smile never materialized. He'd come to save his child and instead he'd as good as signed his death warrant. He turned away, anger rising in his throat.

Julia had to know how high the stakes were. Or did she? Would it be kinder to let her hold on to hope for as long as possible? He joined her where she'd stopped to study the last portrait in line. A young man of about eighteen, decked out in full regalia, including a crown. "Federico," Julia said.

As he stared at his half brother's face, Will tried to identify any feelings he might have and came up only with regret. Regret they'd never met, sure. But also regret the kid had killed himself on a mountain, setting in motion so much death and destruction.

"Your portrait should be up there, too," Julia said.

"Are you sad you aren't going to be queen of Montivitz?"

She looked at him and smiled. "No. You sad you're not going to be a king?"

"Are you kidding?"

"But there was a moment when you considered it, wasn't there?"

"A split second."

She turned to face him. "I'm sorry about your father."

"It doesn't matter. The man is a stranger." He put his hands on her shoulders and added, "Things look bad, Julia. I'd move heaven and earth to spare you the next few hours, but I can't think of a thing I can do."

"It's okay, Will."

He shook his head. Okay? Hardly. He added, "I want you to know I love you. There, I said it. I thought I was in love before, but it wasn't like this. It wasn't as complete or as scary or as exhilarating. I know we haven't known each other long, but I can't help feeling I now understand what real love is. It's selfless. It's bigger than the two people involved. It's you."

A smile, so dazzling it outshone all the painted rubies, sapphires, diamonds and emeralds in the portraits behind her, lit her face. "I love you, too," she whispered. "I've been so afraid for so long, for years and years. I've felt abandoned and unloved and unworthy. I've lied to myself about my own life and now I don't need to lie anymore, and it's because of you. So that now when I should be the most afraid I've ever been, I'm at peace."

"If it was possible, I would marry you right now," he said. Reaching behind her head, he unfastened her hair, watching as it cascaded onto her shoulders. He cupped her face with his hands and dove into her eyes.

"I want you to know how much I would have loved having a life with you," he whispered. "Seeing you pregnant. Raising Leo and our other children together, being the family you never had, building you a beautiful house full of sunshine and laughter and worshipping you until the day you died. I'm sorry I got you into this mess. But I can't say that I'm not grateful to have had the chance to be with you."

"And I would marry you," she said, taking his hands and holding them to her breast. "With you and Leo, I feel a part of something bigger and better, as though I've come home and never want to leave again. I want to give you what you've given me. Security. Love…"

"You heard Poletier. You know what's coming," he murmured.

"I just kind of hoped he might come through in the end," she whispered.

"I should have pushed him off the damn cliff this morning."

"Yes. Well, hindsight—"

The door burst open and Poletier strode into the room, flanked by guards. Will's hands bunched into fists as Julia rushed to the settee and picked up Leo.

"I'm personally escorting you to our prison," the old man said, grinding to a halt. "We are a fair people. There will be a trial."

Poletier handed them back their passports as well as an extra one for an infant named Leonardo Poletier. "You upset my house-keeper today leaving the way you did. She didn't know about that old passage. She thought you had vanished into thin air. Keep your passports on your persons."

"So our bodies can be identified?" It galled Will to have his son identified as related to Poletier. He could just imagine the outpouring of sympathy the baby's cruel death would illicit from the citizens of Montivitz who didn't know the truth. He said, "Is it to be thought we kidnapped my son?"

"The passport identifies him as Albert's son," Poletier said.

Julia said, "Leave Leo with Renee. A prison is no place for an infant."

"Julia is right," Will said, though he knew they would never actually reach the prison. Swallowing the intense desire to have his child's destiny in his control as long as possible, he added, "Leave Leo with Renee."

Poletier nodded at one of the guards who snatched Leo from Julia's resisting arms. Another pointed a gun at Julia's head.

"The child goes with you," he said.

Another walk, this one ending in a huge courtyard where a long black limousine sat idling. It was dark and windy outside, something that surprised Will who had stopped thinking in terms of time of day. What perfect sailing weather! If he and Julia and Leo had made it aboard the *Marie Antoinette,* they'd be headed toward safety, not death.

They were herded into the backseat of the car, Leo handed to Will almost as an afterthought. Two armed guards also climbed into the back, facing them on jump seats, guns trained on Julia and Leo. Poletier slid into the front seat, a driver took the wheel.

Will kissed Leo's forehead then looked at Julia who stared at Leo with such longing that he handed her his baby. She cuddled him close to her breast, tucking the blanket around his legs. His son still slept.

Will thought, *My hands are free. So what? Who do I sacrifice? Leo? Julia? And even if I managed to save one of them, there are two guards, two guns.*

The ride down the cliff gave a clear vista of the city below. Isolated fires sent orange flames dancing into the night sky.

"Bless Paul Bernard's black heart," Poletier said in English. "Thanks to him, your deaths will be attributed to terrorism."

"Tell me why you didn't just kill Aunt Fiona and me from the get-go," Will said. "Why the years of pretend threats and hiding?"

Poletier's smile flashed from the front seat. He had turned to face them. Looking between the two guards' shoulders, he said, "I thought I might need you someday. I kept your aunt too busy and too afraid to ever make trouble. She always thought the king was breathing down your neck."

"Until Federico was born."

"Who knew Theodore would ever get around to marrying and producing a legitimate heir? The man pined for your dead mother and her lost baby for years."

"And then Federico died."

"Stupid boy. On the other hand, once he died, I realized the time was right for my family to lay claim to the throne. Albert had the foresight to marry Renee, whose mother is a distant cousin of your father's. Once you and your son are dead, Albert's claim to the throne will be assured. The people love him."

"Do they know he's a murderer?"

"Now, now. Albert no more murdered anyone than you did. The man who drove the boat armed with a bomb aimed at killing you was a derelict glad for some spare change, not knowing the bomb was controlled from a shoreline remote. The thug who blew up Miss Sheridan's house and tried to kill her would have been well paid if he hadn't been such an idiot. The other man hired to visit your aunt and make sure she didn't cause any trouble was the same man with the remote, by the way, and the same one who 'fixed' your wife's steering column, causing her fatal accident. All useful and you will be pleased to know, all now dead."

"So who sent the man to kill us in Toulon?" Julia asked.

"I did. I knew the moment your plane landed in Paris. The police say he shot himself with his own gun. Clumsy oaf."

Clumsy oaf. The life-and-death struggle in the parking lot reduced to ham-fisted clumsiness. The death of a man, albeit a monster, his broken rib and Julia's gashed face no more than minor annoyances.

"Leo was supposed to die with his mother," Poletier volunteered. "Once he survived, I thought his bloodline might come in useful if Albert's claim is disputed. After all, at that point, I assumed you were dead and your son was an orphan. Renee has a tender spot for children. It gave me quite a start when you called me, not quite dead after all. Not yet, anyway. I knew you would come to Montivitz to save your son.

You Americans are so sentimental, so predictable."

The car rolled into town. Groups of men roamed the streets, flickering firelight casting their silhouettes onto buildings. The sounds of gunfire and shattering glass reached as far as the interior of the luxurious car.

"You have a riot on your hands," Will said.

"Most of it fueled by insiders. The few true dissidents like Paul Bernard will be rounded up once the public is sick of their antics. The citizens will thank the palace for cleaning up Montivitz right before tourist season gets under way. By this time next week, Bernard will be dead, his usefulness outlived."

"So what happens to us now?" Julia said, her voice firm but higher pitched than normal. Will squeezed her hand.

"You have been seen by too many people. Any minute now, this car will be ambushed. Bernard's men will get the credit—and the blame—for your deaths along with those of these other men."

"Just you will survive," Will said.

"As you say."

Will glanced at the guards, one after the

other. Both remained stone-faced, oblivious to what awaited them.

Poletier turned back in his seat and issued more unintelligible orders. The car made a few more turns before coming to a stop in an alley. Poletier said something else to the driver and got out of the car. He walked a short way and turned into an open doorway. The limo's headlights illuminated the empty alley ahead.

Will looked at Julia again. He knew what was coming and so did she. He reached out to touch her face, to touch Leo one last time right as a van turned into the alley and roared up to the limousine. The driver and guards prepared to leave the car. Hands on door handles, feet shifting position, bodies slightly turned. They thought they had time to escape what was coming.

Instead, a blast of gunfire erupted from the van. A microsecond later, the driver slumped over the wheel, the windshield in front of his face shattered into a million pieces.

Will flung himself sideways, pushing Julia down on the seat, throwing himself on top of her and Leo as bullets riddled the car, exploding glass all around them. He knew his body couldn't protect them for long. He knew that sooner or later they would die right as they lay. If he couldn't do more than prolong their life another few seconds, then that was what he would do.

The first bullet hit him a second later.

THE HAIL of bullets stopped at last. Julia opened her eyes to find Will's face pressed against her own. Muffled cries came from Leo, caught between them.

"Will?"

He slowly pushed himself away, dislodging an avalanche of safety glass from his back. When his face contorted with pain, Julia looked for an injury. Bright red blood stained his left sleeve.

"You're hurt," she said.

He more or less fell back onto the seat when his arm gave out on him. "Not as badly as those two," he said, offering his good hand to Julia to help her sit.

As she comforted Leo, she took in the two guards, both slumped over in their seats. One man's head was all but blown away. The other man's chin rested on his chest, his bloody fingers cupping the grip of his handgun.

Will reached forward to retrieve the

weapon. Julia held her breath. Leo stopped crying, either worn out from the effort or distracted by his father's motion.

Will picked the gun up by the barrel and turned it in his hand. Just in time, too, for the guard he'd disarmed wasn't quite as dead as he'd looked.

He grabbed for the gun. Will drew it back but didn't fire. The guard flung himself against his seat, blinking his eyes, raising his hands in a gesture of surrender. He finally said, "Sorry about that. Instinct, you know."

It took Julia a heartbeat to realize he'd spoken perfect English.

"Who are you?" Will demanded.

"CIA," the man said.

"As in Central Intelligence Agency? You're kidding?"

The man produced a tight smile. "Don't forget it's our air base at the center of this mess," he said, brushing glass from his uniform. "We have to protect our interests. Appreciate it if you didn't blow my cover." Taking in Will's condition, he added, "Your arm is a mess, Mr. Wellspring. Is it true you're the king's son?"

"No," Will said, his voice hoarse and full of pain. "Poletier has it all wrong."

"I see." Gesturing at the gun, he added, "I believe you're an architect, right? I may have more time logged in at the firing range than you."

Will handed the gun back to the agent. In the next instant, the back door flew open and a face they'd only seen in posters peered in at them. Fierce black eyes, unruly black curls, a mustache dominating the lower half of his face. Paul Bernard, surrounded by a band of hard looking and heavily armed men. "Everybody out," he demanded.

Julia clutched Leo even tighter as she picked her way out of the car. The CIA agent came next, leaning back in to assist Will. Will stood on his own, his arm dangling at his side. Blood dripped from his fingertips.

With prodding, the agent handed over his gun. Bernard said something Julia couldn't understand. The agent responded with a flood of words, a little groveling, and a hasty and unmolested retreat up the alley.

"You let him go," Julia said, a tiny flicker of hope igniting her heart. If the agent knew Bernard had them, might he not begin negotiations to free them? Maybe they would live to see the sunrise after all.

"I have no issue with some hapless

working man, employee of the palace or not," Bernard said, his English deeply accented. He added, "The escaped guard will be a witness that we were not behind this attack, that it was staged by the palace. He's worth more to us alive than dead." He motioned at a large van that had pulled up behind the limo. "As for you two—you're coming with me."

"Let Miss Sheridan and the baby go," Will said. "They're not important—"

"I'm aware this child is in line to the throne," Paul Bernard snapped. "Hurry, we must leave."

They had to step around a prone body lying by the rear bumper. Poletier, a single shot fired through his forehead. Julia gasped.

Bernard grabbed Julia's arm and hurried her along. "Do not mourn him," he said. "He does not deserve it."

Will, standing outside the van, looked back. "If you didn't have anything to do with this attack, then how did you know we were here?"

"Renee Poletier. She was worried about your son."

"What about her husband? Does he know she's responsible for his father's death?"

"Renee's marriage is not one born of love. To Albert, she is little more than a commodity. Don't worry about her. She is no longer at the palace. And Albert will not live to see morning."

"Good," Will said.

"Get in the van," Bernard repeated, the edge to his voice causing new flickers of alarm in Julia's stomach. Bernard and a few of his men climbed in with them.

The van backed out of the alley at a screaming pace, then turned. Julia wasn't sure in which direction they headed but it seemed to be inland. While Leo fussed, Julia insisted she unwind some of the ace bandage from around Will's ribs to tie around his injured arm. Not as a tourniquet, but they needed to apply pressure or he was in danger of bleeding to death.

Of course, that might be the least of their problems. Her suggestion they detour to a hospital was met with stony silence from both men.

The van eventually rolled through open metal gates and out onto the tarmac of a small airport.

"This strip is adjacent to the American base," Bernard said as the van came to a stop under a pool of overhead light. The guards jumped out. Bernard closed the door after them. He sat facing them, elbows on bent knees.

"I know who you are," Bernard said to Will. "I know you are Lévesque's bastard son. With Federico dead, you are heir to the throne. With Poletier dead, Albert in our custody and your father going mad, you pose a great threat to an independent Montivitz."

Will said, "How do you know about me?"

"Renee Poletier. She is a friend of my sister's. She told us of your existence when she returned from America with your son. She found out about you after Federico died and Poletier and Albert hatched this plan."

Julia looked out the window. A gleaming white Cessna Citation turboprop stood on the tarmac at the edge of the light, a symbol of freedom to Julia, so close she could see the dark outline of the pilot in the cockpit. The door behind the pilot's seat extended down, forming stairs, the inside of the aircraft a glowing rectangle of safety. Was Paul Bernard about to shoot them and fly off to hide somewhere?

Bernard said, "Do you want the crown?"

Julia's gaze swiveled back to Will.

"From what I've seen, Montivitz would be better served by a democracy," he said. "That said, I have to add that as an American citizen, I hope you and your followers will reconsider closing the air base."

"In the end, the people of my country will make that decision at the polls," Bernard said with utter conviction. He pulled at his mustache as he stared at Will who met his gaze with unblinking strength. "How am I to believe you are willing to turn away what every man wants?" Bernard said at last.

"And what's that?" Will asked.

"Power. Wealth. Influence."

"I don't know about every man," Will said. "But what I want is right here beside me. This woman. This baby. The freedom from ever looking over my shoulder again. Peace. Happiness. Self-determination. That's what I want. That's all I want."

Bernard stared at him for a moment longer before breaking into a grin. The expression was more alarming than comforting.

"Poletier said many of the people joining your rebellion are employed by the king," Julia said. "Infiltrators, spies."

"We know this," Bernard said. "Though the numbers are not as great as Poletier imagined."

One of the guards knocked on the window with the shaft of his rifle and yelled something. Bernard swiveled in his seat. Julia, following the direction of his gaze, saw two sets of approaching headlights still some distance away but closing fast.

"Go," Bernard said, opening the door and all but pushing Julia and Leo outside. Will joined them. The wind whipped hair and clothes. Leo began to cry in earnest. Other than holding him close, there was little Julia could do to comfort him.

"The plane will take you to Italy. Don't ever come back to Montivitz. Go fast… Poletier's men are coming." With that, he and his men jumped back into the van and drove away. One set of lights veered off in pursuit.

Will's hand closed over Julia's arm and they took off, Julia shifting Leo's weight to her hip. The car came closer, shots rang out, bullets hit the tarmac. Julia flew to the plane and up the stairs, turning to help Will.

But Will wasn't there. Instead he lay on the ground thirty feet away, clutching his left leg. Waving with his good arm, he yelled, "Go, go." His voice was almost inaudible over the sound of the plane engine and Leo's terrified screams in Julia's ear.

The pilot reached around her, trying to close the door. He took a bullet in his shoulder and staggered backward.

Time stopped. No sound. Nothing.

This was it. This was the moment those dreadful premonitions had been leading up to. Will had taken them this far. Now it was her turn. She had to close this door and fly Leo to safety, regardless of Will's fate.

It was up to her to save Leo. Will couldn't.

These thoughts passed through her head in a blinding instant and then were gone.

The wounded pilot shouted at her in an unintelligible language. She slapped his face, gaining his attention, then shoved Leo against him. He took the child with his good arm, looking too surprised to do anything else.

In the next moment, she ran down the stairs and across the tarmac, knelt beside Will and hoisted him to his feet with a strength she never knew she possessed. His torn jeans were stained with his blood. He looped his unwounded arm around her neck and they stumbled toward the plane, their assailants' car now close enough that gunfire and bullets whizzed all around them.

Julia shoved Will up the stairs, following as bullets hit metal. She pounded the button to close the door before helping Will sag into a seat. Then she dashed forward.

The pilot, face pale and shoulder bloody, had taken his place in the cockpit, flipping switches and trying to control Leo's squirming, wiggling body with only one hand.

Julia plucked the baby from his lap as the pilot started the plane rolling. She moved swiftly aft, placing Leo in his father's loving arms. They both looked up at her, one red faced and hysterical, the other somber.

"You came back for me," Will said, catching her hand.

"Of course I came back for you." She leaned over and kissed his fingers. "I've waited twenty years for a family. No way I'm going to leave half of it behind."

"Damn straight," he said with a lopsided grin followed by a painful grimace.

She picked up the diaper bag she'd thrown aside when first entering the plane, dug out a diaper and handed it to him. "Keep pressure on your leg," she said.

"I will."

One more stolen moment to drink in the sight of them. Her bleeding, shot-up, rib-cracked lover and his screeching, petrified baby boy.

Her family.

Sure, there were a few hurdles to overcome. A few legal issues. A few suspicious deaths, blown-up possessions, lost identities, things like that. For instance, what would her married name be? Wellspring? Chastain? Noble?

Interesting dilemma.

But it would work out.

With a smile of perfect faith and holding on to the back of the seats to steady herself, she made her way to the cockpit to assist the pilot in getting them off the ground and the hell out of Montivitz.

The future awaited.

* * * * *

Melita had been expecting a chaste quick kiss of the generic variety. But this kiss with Sully was the kind that sparked a dying flame to life. The kind of kiss you can't plan for. The kind of kiss memories are built on.

The memory of her murdered lover, Nemo, came to her then and she made a starved little noise in the back of her throat. She raised her arms and threaded her fingers through Sully's hair, pulled him closer. Felt his body settle, then melt into her.

In that instant her hunger for him grew, and his for her. She pressed herself to him with more urgency, and he responded in kind.

Melita came out of her kiss-induced memory of Nemo with a start. "Wait a minute." She pushed Sully away from her. "You bastard!"

She spit two nasty words at him in Greek, then wiped his kiss from her lips.

"I thought you deserved some solid proof that I'm still in one piece." He started for the door. "The clock's ticking, honey. Come on, let's get out of here."

"That's it? You sucker me into kissing you, and that's all you have to say?"

"I'm sorry. How's that?"

He didn't sound sorry in the least. "You're—"

"Getting out of this godforsaken prison cell. Stop whining and let's go."

"Not if I was being shot at sunrise. Go. You deserve whatever you get if you walk out that door."

He turned back. "Freedom is what I'm going to get."

"A second of freedom before the guards in the hall shoot you." She jammed her hands on her hips. "And to think I was worried about you."

"If you're staying behind, it's no skin off my ass."

"Wait! What about our deal?"

"You just said you're not coming. Make up your mind."

"Have you forgotten we need a boat?"

"How could I? You keep harping on it."

"I'm not going without a boat. And those guards out there aren't going to just let you walk out of here. You need me and we need a plan."

"I already have a plan. I'm getting out of here. That's the plan."

"I should have realized that you never intended to take me with you from the very beginning. You're a liar and a coward."

Of everything she had read, there was nothing in Sully Paxton's file that hinted he was a coward, but it was the one word that seemed to register in that one-track mind of his. The look he nailed her with a second later was pure venom.

He came at her so quickly she didn't have time to get out of his way. "You know I'm not a coward."

"Prove it. Give me until dawn. I need one more night to put everything in place before we leave the island."

"You're asking me to stay in this cell one more night...and trust you?"

"Yes."

He snorted. "Yesterday you knew they were planning to harm me, but instead of doing something about it you went to bed and never gave me a second thought. Suppose tonight you do the same. By tomorrow I might damn well be in my grave."

"Okay, I screwed up. I won't do it again." Melita sucked in a ragged breath. "I can't leave this minute. Dawn, Sully. Wait until dawn." When he looked as if he was about to say no, she pleaded, "Please wait for me."

"You're asking a lot. The door's open now. I would be a fool to hang around here and trust that you'll be back."

"What you can trust is that I want off this island as badly as you do, and you're my only hope."

"I must be crazy."

"Is that a yes?"

"Dammit!" He turned his back on her. Swore twice more.

"You won't be sorry."

He turned around. "I already am. How about we seal this new deal?"

He was staring at her lips. Suddenly

Melita knew what he expected. "We already sealed it."

"One more. You enjoyed it. Admit it."

"I enjoyed it because I was kissing someone else."

He laughed. "That's a good one."

"It's true. It might have been your lips, but it wasn't you I was kissing."

"If that's your excuse for wanting to kiss me, then—"

"I was kissing Nemo."

"What's a nemo?"

Melita gave Sully a look that clearly told him that he was trespassing on sacred ground. She was about to enforce it with a warning when a voice in the hall jerked them both to attention.

She bolted away from the wall. "Get back in bed. Hurry. I'll be here before dawn."

She didn't reach the door before he snagged her arm, pulled her up against him and planted a kiss on her lips that took her completely by surprise.

When he released her, he said, "If you're confused about who just kissed you, the name's Sully. I'll be here waiting at dawn. Don't be late."

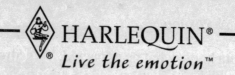

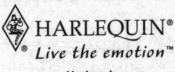

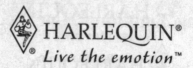

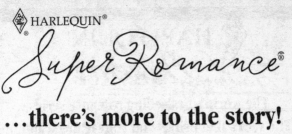
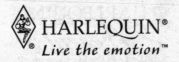

HARLEQUIN®
Presents~

The world's bestselling romance series...
The series that brings you your favorite authors,
month after month:

Helen Bianchin...Emma Darcy
Lynne Graham...Penny Jordan
Miranda Lee...Sandra Marton
Anne Mather...Carole Mortimer
Susan Napier...Michelle Reid

and many more uniquely talented authors!

Wealthy, powerful, gorgeous men...
Women who have feelings just like your own...
The stories you love, set in exotic, glamorous locations...

HARLEQUIN®
Presents~

Seduction and Passion Guaranteed!

Harlequin® Historical
Historical Romantic Adventure!

*Imagine a time of chivalrous
knights and unconventional ladies,
roguish rakes and impetuous
heiresses, rugged cowboys
and spirited frontierswomen—
these rich and vivid tales will
capture your imagination!*

*Harlequin Historical . . .
they're too good to miss!*

SPECIAL EDITION™

Emotional, compelling stories that capture the intensity of living, loving and creating a family in today's world.

Desire

Modern, passionate reads that are powerful and provocative.

nocturne

Dramatic and sensual tales of paranormal romance.

Romantic SUSPENSE

Romances that are sparked by danger and fueled by passion.